A Christmas Present

Book Eleven of the
Coming Back to Cornwall series

Katharine E. Smith

HEDDON PUBLISHING

First edition published in 2024 by Heddon Publishing.

ISBNs
Paperback 978-1-913166-94-6
Ebook 978-1-913166-95-3

Cover by Catherine Clarke Design
www.catherineclarkedesign.co.uk

www.heddonpublishing.com
www.facebook.com/heddonpublishing

Katharine E. Smith is the author of twenty novels. *A Christmas Present* is the eleventh Coming Back to Cornwall book and Katharine promises to never again say that she's finished writing this popular series. The Connections books are also set in Cornwall, with each story focusing on a different character but each tale linked inextricably to the others. Katharine's most recent series is What Comes Next and is set – for a change – in Shropshire, where she lives with her husband, their two children, and two excitable dogs.

A Philosophy graduate, Katharine initially worked in the IT and charity sectors. She turned to freelance editing in 2009, which led to her setting up Heddon Publishing, working with independent authors across the globe.

You can find details of her books on her website: www.katharineesmith.com

Information about her work with other authors can be found here:
www.heddonpublishing.com
and here:
www.heddonbooks.com

For the Biscuit Chatterers
– Helena, Lisa and Laura –
Christmas is all about the biscuits.

A Christmas Present

So this is Christmas. This year it is going to be just the four of us… five, if you count our dog Meg, and I do. I can't pretend this would have been my first choice for how we spend the day – I am used to busy, bustling Christmases with lots of family and friends – but as time has gone by, I've begun to come round to the idea.

Since the summer it's felt as though, one by one, my family and best friends have revealed that they won't be around this year. It's like a disappointing advent calendar: behind each door is another revelation.

Mum and Dad were first, having decided they want to go on a Christmas cruise again, as they did a few years back.

"You don't mind do you, love?" asked Mum.

I knew the correct answer. "No, of course not." (I did, a bit.)

Sam's mum Karen and her partner Ron are going to be staying with my sister-in-law Janie and my ex-colleague and lovely friend Jonathan, in Spain.

"You don't mind do you, my loves?" asked Karen.

We knew the correct answer. "No, of course not." (I didn't, or not much.)

Julie, Luke and Zinnia are of course having a Canadian Christmas in their new home. Julie's mum and brother and his partner and her little boy are flying out to see them.

"You should come too!" Julie said.

I'd laughed. "I think that might be a bit too much, and I'm sure Cherry and Lee would prefer it to be a family thing."

"You are family!" Julie had protested.

"Well, yeah…" It's true. Julie has been in my life since we were eleven years old. She's like my sister as much as my best friend. Luke is Sam's best friend and I love him dearly, and as for Zinnia, she's like a cousin to Holly and Ben. I miss them all so much that I ache sometimes but we haven't yet been out to visit them, for a variety of reasons.

It's Kate's turn to have Sophie this year – although really Sophie is getting a little bit old for having to do alternate Christmases with her parents – and we will all miss her but I know she'll have a great time in Devon with Kate and Isaac and her little brother Jacob.

David and Martin and their kids – and Bea – will be staying with Martin's brother, who recently moved to Derbyshire.

We really are going to be on our own.

After so many busy, hectic, loud and lively Christmases it will be nice to have a quiet one. Just us five. That's what I keep telling myself anyway.

1

"My god, I'd love a quiet one, just me and Paul." Shona and I are on a video call, although she is only a few miles away from here. I can see the view from the floor-to-ceiling window behind her – the grey and restless sea. "We've got both Paul's kids, and my dad, and Paul's dad – and you know they don't get on. That's just for starters. Georgia and Lenny are both bringing 'partners', who we've never met. My god, those kids' relationships last no longer than a gnat's wheeze. And why do I feel like I'm going to end up doing everything? Oh that's right, because I always do. I asked Si and Lydia if I could come with them to St Lucia but apparently three's a crowd…"

Si is our honorary celebrity friend, only because he's madly in love with Lydia, who used to work for me at the Sail Loft Hotel. He's a much sought-after actor (sought after by film producers and half the country's adult female population) and Shona has been working as his agent for over a year now, having brought me in to manage much of her PR business.

"You mean they don't want to share their exclusive swim-up villa with super-super-super king-sized bed and all-inclusive room service with you?"

"No. Funny that. Still, it doesn't sound exactly Christmassy, does it? I'd much rather be here. With Paul. And his kids. And my dad. And Paul's dad…"

"Yeah right!" I snort, and we both laugh.

I imagine being somewhere like St Lucia with Sam over Christmas… I can but dream. Having said that, while Ben and Holly are still small, I do like being at home over the holidays. We've had some lovely Christmases, the most memorable when Holly made her early appearance. And she is not yet old enough to feel aggrieved that her birthday is swallowed up by the big day. She just believes herself to be double-special, and long may that feeling last.

"Anyway my dear, we'd better crack on with some work," says Shona.

"We had," I say, as enthusiastically as possible. I miss being my own boss – and I miss Amethi, and Julie, always – but I am also grateful to be able to work flexibly, particularly when one of the kids is ill, or Holly has a diabetes clinic to attend; a regular feature in our family calendar over the last year and a half.

And it's not that I don't like the work I do for Shona; it is interesting in its own way, and a chance for me to stretch my organisational muscles. Our clients are for the most part lovely, and I enjoy the creative side of PR work as well. But, if I'm honest, it's lonely. I suspect I am spending too much time on my own; my contact with clients and Shona is largely 'virtual', either video calls or emails, which is very handy but lacking in the human contact that can really make a day's work worthwhile. If it wasn't for my walks to and from school with the kids, I might not see another human being from one end of the day to the other and the short daylight hours seem to make each day doubly depressing. I think perhaps with all the changes in my life recently – not to mention the lack of sleep – my self-esteem has taken a bit of a battering.

I know I am a terrible person, complaining when really I am incredibly lucky. I have to give myself a good kick in the behind sometimes, and try to shake it all off. But I do just feel a bit flat.

We worked so hard, me and Julie, to get Amethi to where it was. I know it's a cliché but it was so much more than a business; it was a significant part of my life. I was so proud of what we achieved, and I loved it, and now it's all gone. And not just Amethi, but Julie. That may be the worst of all.

As Shona and I discuss our newest client, What a Pa-lather – an up-and-coming ethical cosmetics firm from Devon – my gaze keeps moving to just beyond Shona's shoulder.

"Are you alright, Alice?"

"What? Oh, yeah, sorry, I'm fine – it's just your backdrop is a bit distracting."

Shona turns her back on me, to admire the view herself. "Oh, yeah, I know. It's mesmerising. I have to work with my back to it or I won't get anything done."

"I can imagine." My background view might also be described as distracting but not so much mesmerising, consisting as it does of a pile of toys and books stacked haphazardly on the IKEA shelves behind me, and a large framed painting of a sunflower against a blue sky, just above a mark on the wall where Ben threw one of his Bakugan toys a little too enthusiastically.

Shona turns back and flashes one of her dazzling smiles my way. "Hey, you know, going back to Christmas, you should come over on Christmas Eve, bring Sam, and Ben and Holly of course."

"Oh, I..."

"Go on," she urges. "Please. I need back-up with all Paul's lot here. And Dad will love you. You can keep him away from Paul's dad."

"Ha!" I laugh. "Well, thank you for the invite. I'll check with Sam." I am not really sure that we want to spend Christmas Eve at Paul and Shona's, with their families not ours, but as I've already divulged to her that all my family and closest friends are otherwise engaged, I don't really have a ready excuse not to.

"Brilliant! OK. I'd better go." I hear a familiar voice in the background. "We're going for a run," she whispers to me and rolls her eyes.

"Rather you than me," I grin, thinking back to the days when I used to go running a couple of times a week, probably burning off the frustration of working at World of Stationery. I carried on for a while, after Julie and I moved down to Cornwall, but somehow it dwindled away and I can't remember the last time I ran anywhere just for the sake of running. It was pre-kids, I can be fairly sure of that. Pre-Amethi, I expect. Maybe I should start again, I muse. But not now.

"Is that Alice?" I hear from the laptop speaker, and Paul Winter's face moves into view, appearing far too close to the screen, as if he's going to kiss me. That ship sailed a long time ago. A potential complication in my working relationship with Shona; she is married to my erstwhile date. But that never really took off and I don't think Shona is bothered. She shouldn't be. Paul is as attractive as ever but we're very different people and besides, I have Sam.

"Hi Paul," I smile.

"Everything OK? Sam and the kids?"

"Yeah, all good thanks." We haven't mentioned our near-miss of a relationship for a long time. Instead of anything romantic, Paul really enabled Julie and me to buy Amethi, and he became a trusted business advisor to us, as well as introducing us to the local networking scene so that we made some amazing connections. So that, I think, was the reason he came into my life; not as an attractive older (much richer) alternative to Sam, as he had seemed at the time. And now it's his wife who is helping me out.

"You have to stop thinking like that," Sam has said to me. "You're helping her out, not the other way round. At the very least, you are of mutual benefit to each other."

I pretend to agree with him but I can't quite seem to shake the feeling that in employing me, Shona is just doing me a favour.

"I invited Alice and Sam and the kids over on Christmas Eve," Shona says to Paul now, tilting her head back to kiss him. I see his chin is stubbled and the stubble is nearly white. "That's OK, isn't it?"

"Of course, of course, the more the merrier," Paul says, with the ease of a man who has to do very little catering or arranging himself.

"I need to check with Sam…" I say but I don't think they are listening.

"Great," Shona says, flashing another smile at the screen. "We'd better be going though, before it gets dark. Don't want to miss the last bit of daylight."

Her face freezes on the screen as she ends the call. Even

with her mouth frozen mid-sentence, she is gorgeous. And she's a good person; and really a very nice boss. She and Paul are made for each other. I look away towards my window, to see that it really is nearly dark out there. It's been one of those grey, muted days that never really seems to get going. I have had the lights on since I started work so I haven't even noticed the daylight fading.

I'd better get moving too, to collect Ben and Holly. When I think back to those pre-motherhood days, and the excess of spare hours I had... I find it hard to believe life used to be like that. I would even get bored sometimes, from having nothing to do. Imagine! I wish I could have banked some of those hours, they'd come in very handy now.

Shona's face has vanished so I save the document I was working on then shut down my laptop. Time to switch from work mode to mum mode. The walk to school always gives me the perfect opportunity to do just that. I enjoy the peace and quiet to put work behind me as I transform from one of my identities to another, and I find myself looking forward to this little segment of time to myself each day. I don't think I will ever tire of the views as I make my way to the top of the town, where the school sits proudly, like a crown. The rows of houses, cascading down towards the beating heart of the harbour, and beyond that the sea, sometimes sapphire-blue and shimmering or, like today, simmering with a grey resentment underneath the heavy sky. I love it in all its guises and I sometimes still can't believe it, after all these years. I actually live here.

I call Meg, who is so slow these days, and I can see she's not going to want to come with me, curled up as she is on her comfy bed. She lifts her greying muzzle to blink at me, then closes her eyes while her head is still in the air.

"That's OK," I say, my eyes surprised by tears at the thought of her age. "I don't blame you. Wish I could curl up with you."

But I cannot. I pull on my coat, and my hat and gloves for good measure. It's not too cold during the days but as soon as the sun's sunk out of sight, it can get decidedly chilly. Locking the door behind me, I start to walk down the road.

"Alice!" I hear, and I inwardly groan. Should I pretend I haven't heard?

But no... footsteps are coming quickly behind me.

"Phew! Caught you!" Natalie, who lives a few houses down the road and whose kids – Bobby and Courtney – are in the years below Ben and Holly, puts a hand on my arm. "Are you walking to school?"

"I am," I confirm.

"Great, I'll walk with you."

No asking if I mind, although of course if she did I am unlikely to say that yes, actually, I do. Natalie is not a bad person, by any means, but it feels like she has latched on to me. She is relatively new here, having moved into our street during the summer, and because our children go to the same school and she has an older boy and a younger girl, she seems to think it means we have a lot in common.

I know it's mean that I am not more welcoming towards her but I just don't always have the energy at the moment, and I try to keep her at arm's length. Natalie is full of nervous energy and one of those people who fires question after question at you so that it doesn't feel like a conversation, more an interview. I sometimes come away from our meetings exhausted. But I should acknowledge that at least she doesn't just talk about herself. I don't really much about her. Her husband Rob is away with work a lot and it seems he supports the family financially, while Natalie does everything else. I fully respect her for that because I know what that 'everything else' entails, but I do also think it means we have less in common.

My days are ruled by my job almost as much as they are by family and for me work is very much part of who I am. Despite all my complaining, I don't think I would like it if I didn't have a job. It allows me to be a grown-up on my own terms and have conversations with people who don't just see me as Ben and Holly's mum.

I fix a smile on my face and ready myself for a different walk to school than I had hoped for. I know I should be pleased that Natalie wants to talk to me, and I do realise she probably needs a few friendly faces around her while she settles in this new place where not everybody is welcoming to incomers; most are but, like in any small town, there are people who are set in their ways and new people can be treated with some suspicion. But it's an effort and in my heart of hearts I wish that she would find somebody else to lean on.

I am not sure I'm my best self these days, in all honesty. I'm a bit fed up. I am tired and short-tempered, from the broken nights' sleep when Holly's blood sugars are playing up, or an abstract worry has taken hold and refuses to let me rest. And, as we have already established, I am finding it difficult having to work for somebody else again and I wish that I still had Amethi to go to. I wish Mum and Dad were here for Christmas. I wish Meg wasn't getting old. I wish Sam was at home more. And on top of all of that, I wish Julie was still here. But I'm old enough to know that, Christmas or not, wishes don't just come true because we want them to.

2

It's beginning to look a lot like Christmas. Despite my lack of cheer, festive or otherwise, it is nice seeing the trees in people's houses and from up near the school you can just glimpse the lights strung along the streets down in town. It provides a bit of brightness on a grey day like today.

"Are you all set for Christmas?" Natalie asks me.

"Erm…" I say. Am I? I suppose so. This year, in fact, I've been more organised than usual. Working with all these great little companies Shona's procured for her PR firm, I have access to lots of beautiful products, often at a reduced rate. I bought all-new Christmas decorations from Baubles Up, who make tree ornaments and garlands and advent calendars from recycled bottles and bags. I have all the kids' stocking-fillers sorted, including cute little soaps and body washes courtesy of What a Pa-lather, handmade chocolates from Choc-a-Block, wooden wind-up toys from Clockwork Porridge, and packs of beautiful playing cards designed by Jenny Urquhart; an artist up in Bristol. Cheese, wine, bread, fruit and veg are all on order from some of the suppliers I used to work with at Amethi, who kindly still supply me even in the small quantities that I need these days.

I've been buying toys and clothes and books when I've seen them throughout the year, so most of the children's presents are sorted. Sam's are bought and paid for too, including tickets for one of the Eden Project gigs next summer, and a night in one of the bell tents on site. Really this is a present for me as well – I already have Mum and Dad lined up to childmind that weekend.

"Getting there," I say to Natalie. "How about you?"

"Oh no, I've got loads to do!" she says, bumping against me. It irritates me, though I don't know why. "I don't know where the time goes, I really don't. It's not like I'm out at work; I'm just at home most days. Which reminds me, you still haven't come round for that cuppa…"

"Oh I know, I'm sorry," I say. "It's just that I'm meant to be working during the school days. It's the only chance I have to concentrate on what I'm doing."

"I suppose it must be," she says. "Well tell you what, why don't you all come round this afternoon? I can do them some tea if you like. And me and you can have a proper sit down and chat."

"That's really kind of you," I say, thinking fast, "but we're going to my parents' after school today."

"Oh." I can see she is disappointed, and I feel bad. "No problem. You are lucky, having family nearby."

"I know. I really am."

"I miss my mum all the time."

"Where is she again?"

"Lincolnshire."

"That is a long way."

"Yes." She looks so sad, I feel suddenly awful, but I can't very well say I lied about going to Mum and Dad's. Can I?

"Look, why don't we do something at the weekend?" I

find myself saying without having thought it through. "Jungle Den or something? Or even the beach if the weather's OK?"

"I'd love that!" Natalie's face lights up and I feel even worse at how such a little thing can apparently make such a difference to her. "But I'll have to check with Rob."

"Great." I feel spots of rain dropping on me and I look up and sigh. "Doesn't feel very Christmassy, does it?"

"Here, get under my umbrella," Natalie says, deftly opening it up and sipping her arm through mine so we are both under shelter.

"Thank you," I say, wondering if I can slip free without seeming rude.

"It'll feel Christmassy soon enough too!" Natalie says. "Just think, it's the Christmas plays next week."

"True."

"Are your two excited? Courtney can't wait. She's going to be a star. I don't mean like the star of the show, she's one of the Twinkling Stars, singing to *Dancing in the Moonlight*."

"Ah, that'll be cute."

"It will, won't it?"

"What's Bobby doing?"

"He's one of the soldiers, like your Ben."

"Of course," I say. Ben is very excited that he is a Roman centurion this year, and he gets to boss around his troops.

As we approach the school I see Becky, whose son Jasper is the same age as Ben. Her husband Andrew is one of Sam's old mates and the two of them run the Beach Bar down on the surfing beach. On New Year's Eve they're having a party there for a few of us as the fancy-dress-filled streets can be a bit overwhelming for the littlest of our children.

"Excuse me Natalie," I say, deftly extricating myself. "I just need to go and have a chat with Becky."

"Oh, sure," she says. "I'd better get round to the reception door anyway. Maybe see you on the way home?"

"Maybe," I say then, remembering my lie, "Oh, but I'm going to Mum and Dad's."

"Of course," she says.

I begin to hurry towards Becky across the playground, which is already dotted with puddles, but I find myself turning back briefly to see Natalie walking around the corner of the school, her bright rainbow-striped umbrella a contrasting pop of colour against the grey sky and the dark brick walls. But despite the flash of brightness, she seems a dejected figure, her shoulders drooping slightly as she makes her way between the little knots of other mums laughing and chatting with each other. I feel a sudden clenching of compassion within me and I'm annoyed at myself for not being a better person.

3

"You didn't say we were going to Granny and Grandad's," says Ben loudly and I glance over my shoulder to make sure Natalie isn't within hearing distance. I feel awful that I lied to her. Why didn't I just accept her kind invitation? I honestly don't know what's wrong with me. Everything just seems like such an effort. It's possible I'm spending so much time on my own I'm forgetting how to be sociable.

"Yes, well I'd forgotten, sorry," I laugh lightly.

"Want to go home," Holly says and I look at her pale, worn face.

It's a long day for a little person and this time of year is especially hard on the kids. There's been a lead-up to Christmas since October when they're given their parts in the various plays, and in fact even before then they are tasked with creating their Christmas pictures which are duly made into Christmas cards and sold to us parents, grandparents, carers, etc. to help raise money for the school PTA. I don't think that the children can cope with much more by the time December comes around and I feel extra bad now that I'm dragging Holly down into town to my parents' and all just to get out of going for a cup of tea at

Natalie's. I just hope Mum and Dad are in. Maybe Dad will give us a lift home if I ask him nicely.

As it is, the walk down to town is interrupted by Holly having a hypo, where her blood sugars have gone low, and we have to stop for a while for her to eat some sweets and then wait for her glucose levels to rise. This is so much easier than it used to be because, instead of having to get out all the kit and do a little finger-prick blood test, thanks to the wonders of technology Holly now has a sensor attached to her arm – which sends her blood glucose reading to her phone, and that in turn sends it to mine and Sam's. So now I can just check my screen to see when her blood sugar is rising again. Even so it's not ideal and of course the rain decides to increase its strength as we wait. Not having an umbrella, we try to take shelter next to a garden wall. This serves me right for lying to Natalie, I think, though it doesn't seem fair that Ben and Holly should suffer. Still, it gives me the chance to message Mum and check that she and Dad are in.

Yes, of course! We'd love to see you. You can help persuade Dad that we need to put the tree up. And I can make you all some tea if you like. Or just the kids, if you're eating with Sam later xx

I feel immediately better but then Natalie pops into my head again, how she said she is missing her mum. It must be hard for her. Still, I can't do anything about that.

Once Holly's face has some colour and we confirm that the sweets have done their job and her blood glucose is now a healthy 4.9 and rising, I heft the school bags onto my shoulder and take my children's hands in mine then we hurry down the rain-soaked streets, car headlights reflecting on the shining surfaces and bouncing off windows. The star on the church spire is bright amidst the downpour and even in this weather the town looks perfect to me, the harbour with its Christmas lights just visible across the orange-lichened rooftops. Down in the heart of things, the entire length of Fore Street is adorned with strings of lights and I imagine people stepping gratefully into the shops, putting down umbrellas, trying not to drip water everywhere.

I breathe it in, the vague scent of salt and seaweed and fish on the air. Despite everything, it makes me smile.

"Come on Mummy!" Holly says, breaking into a run and dragging me down the hill.

"Careful!" I laugh, worried I'll slip and fall. "I'm not as nimble as you."

Ben lets go of my hand and saunters as best he can behind us; a casual, cool eight-year-old, hoping any observers won't link him with his silly little sister and even sillier old mum. But Holly is laughing and screaming as she splashes through the puddles and it's catching, her joy. Who cares that it's raining? It's just water. And here I am, hand in hand with my nearly-six-year-old girl, running downhill towards my parents' house in this most beautiful of towns. All thoughts of Natalie behind me for now, I laugh out loud and by the time we reach Mum and Dad's house I need to bend over, to catch my breath. I'm too hot now in my hat and gloves and Holly isn't the only one with colour in her cheeks.

***

"Here we go." Dad brings in a plate of biscuits and a pot of tea while Mum follows on with glasses of juice, a jug of milk and three mugs. In the hallway, our soaked-through coats are hanging on hooks above the radiator. I imagine great clouds of steam rising from them while they dry.

"Thank you," I sigh, sinking back into the chair and putting my feet up on the footstool. There is nothing like a visit to Mum and Dad to put things right.

The kids are busily putting together a train track Mum bought in the charity shop, and all I have to do is sit and relax, and let the day wash over me.

"How was work?" Mum asks.

"Oh, you know… the same old," I say.

"But it's still OK?"

"Oh, yeah, no it's great thanks." I don't really want to talk about work now. It is OK. It is great. But it's not my dream. Then again, how many people consider their jobs their dream? Not many, I am pretty sure of that. "Anyway, what about this tree?"

"What tree?" Dad asks. He looks from me to Mum. "Oh I see, you've been getting Alice on side, have you?"

"Yes. Well Alice understands, don't you love?"

I just smile and look at Dad.

"I don't see the point of putting it up when we're away over Christmas. We won't get back till the day before New Year's Eve then we'll just have to take it down again."

"Don't be such a misery, Phil!" says Mum. "I bet Ben and Holly would like to decorate our tree, wouldn't you kids?"

"Yes!" exclaims Holly.

Ben gives a pretend-cool shrug. "Sure."

"Sue!" Dad is mock-annoyed. "I see I'm outnumbered. Go on then. I give in."

Mum and I grin at each other.

The hot tea warms me from the inside and Mum insists that I sit and 'unwind' while she and Dad and the kids put up the tree and unpack the decorations. They exclaim over the ones I made when I was a child and I roll my eyes but I am secretly pleased they've kept them. The joy of being an only child, I suppose. They treasured everything. I, meanwhile, am hoping to keep our tree minimalist this year with only my new Baubles Up decorations. I think it's a side effect of my new line of work. Everything is so stylised; it has to be, but it's starting to seep into my life.

Dad puts some Christmas carols on and he's soon in the spirit. I take some photos of the four of them hanging the shining stars and spinning tops on the branches, then one of Dad lifting Holly to place the angel at the top.

"My little Christmas angel," Dad says to Holly and she wraps her arms round his neck, pressing against his face. I take another photo. Some of these will be nice framed, maybe as a little extra present for Mum and Dad.

Mum does fish fingers and chips for Ben and Holly and she works out the carb content for Holly's insulin. She has become quite the pro in this regard and she does it now almost without thinking. It's dark outside and Dad draws the curtains against the rain, which is still battering the windows.

It's funny to think I used to live in this house and now my parents live here. It has been host to some key moments for me and I sometimes like to wander around, particularly if I have the place to myself, and remember them all. That night when Sam turned up; it was raining then too, though it was summer rain and quite different. Nevertheless, he'd been shivering and I had run him a bath, which we ended up sharing… My mind sinks back into those bubbles from so many years ago.

When did we last have a bath together? I don't even know. That's how life goes, isn't it? We fill it up with more and more: work and kids; rent, mortgages, insurance; parents' evenings and ferrying children to swimming lessons and birthday parties, and all the other responsibilities which come with growing up. The hedonistic, joyful times just gradually slip away as we have less and less time to ourselves. But the romance and the thrill and excitement at the beginning of a relationship; weren't they a lead-up to this? A precursor to settling down, to starting a family?

Would I want to swap everything I have now to get those times back? No, I would not. I would not give up what I have now for anything – but I wouldn't mind a little taste of those carefree days again, even just occasionally.

"I made mince pies earlier!" Dad says proudly, bearing a plate of them before him once the children have finished eating.

"Kids? Mince pies for pudding?"

"Don't like mince pies," Holly says, predictably.

"Yes please, Grandad," says Ben.

"Alice?"

"Go on then," I say, helping myself to one and taking a bite. They are still warm and the pastry is perfectly crumbly with a snow-scattering of icing sugar glinting across the surface. "These are good, Dad! You're missing out, Holly."

She pouts.

"Don't worry love, you can have a yoghurt," Mum says,

bustling off to get her one. It doesn't take much to put a smile on my daughter's face again, but I can see she's tired.

"Then we'd better be getting going," I say. "I wonder if it's still raining…"

"You're not walking home at this time of night!" Dad says, as I thought he might. "I'll give you a lift."

"Yes!" Ben says.

"Yes!" Holly copies.

Yes! I think.

So we pile into Dad's car, Ben and Holly in their seats, which have become a permanent fixture in the back. I sit next to Dad and he fiddles with the radio. The wipers are going ten-to-the-dozen as we travel up the steep hill but we are at our house in a handful of minutes and I'm pleased to see the lights are on and Sam's car is in the driveway.

"I won't come in," says Dad. "Give my best to Sam, and we'll see you at the weekend."

"Great," I say, then I think, *Oh bugger*. I'd said to Natalie about getting together at the weekend but it's Mum and Dad's Christmas party on Saturday, before they leave for their holiday on Monday. Damn.

As Dad drives off I glance down the street and see that Natalie's house is in darkness except for one upstairs window. There is no car on their drive. Rob must be out at work still. Maybe Natalie's taken the opportunity for an early night. I'll have to see if we can do Jungle Den another time. I hope she won't mind.

"Daddy!" Holly shrieks as the door opens and there, in the doorway, which sheds its golden light outside to welcome us home, is Sam. Tall and gorgeous as always. Holly runs at him and wraps her arms round his legs. Even Ben offers a hug. Then the children are running into the house, transferring their love to Meg, who has plodded to the hallway, happily accepting their cuddles. It leaves me free to put my own arms around Sam and kiss him – which I do, slowly.

"What's that for?" he asks, smiling.

"Just because I love you," I say, and he puts his arms around me, pulling me into the warmth and closing the door behind me, shutting out the darkness and the rain.

4

On Saturday, we get to Mum and Dad's just before lunchtime, before anyone else arrives. They've invited the usual suspects: Karen, Ron, David, Martin, Esme, Tyler, Bea... then there are Craig and Diane, who run a bouncy castle hire company and a hairdresser's. We first met Craig when he moved down here and was struggling with his mental health. He initially suffered some unhelpful remarks from some of the locals, and he took them to heart, but he's proved himself again and again as an asset to the town, and I think it is safe to say that with Diane by his side he's now bedded in.

Mum and Dad have also invited a few friends of theirs from their days running the Sail Loft and, because of Dad's place on the town council, my parents have come to know a few of the other local dignitaries – I call them that to wind them up – so there are a couple of former town mayors in attendance too.

Dad's been hard at work perfecting his mince pies – it turns out we were guinea pigs the other day and Mum tells me he's made a batch every day this week. "Meanwhile I've been making sausage rolls and vol-au-vents, mini pasties – veggie versions as well as meat, don't worry – potato salad and coleslaw, jam tarts and chocolate brownies…" Mum gestures to the table in the dining room which has been pushed back against the wall to make space for the guests to mingle, and to act as a buffet table. It looks beautiful, with sprigs of berried holly and battery-powered tealights tucked between bowls and platters. There is a huge cheese board and two boxes of crackers, along with a roll of thick yellow butter with a knife lying enticingly across it, awaiting permission to slice its way through.

"I bet Sue's done a proper spread," Julie had said wistfully on a WhatsApp call last night.

"She will have done," I agreed.

"Maybe that's what I should do! British Buffets," Julie's face lit up. She's been trying to think of a new way to earn a living; one that she can fit around Zinnia.

"It's got a ring to it," I said. "But would they really go for it in Canada? Surely all that stuff just seems weird outside the UK. It does seem like it's dying out here though. Maybe there would actually be a market for it. Retro buffets."

"Yes!" Julie exclaimed. "Alice, you should do it. That's pretty much your level of cooking."

"Hey!" I said, mock-indignantly. "Now you're not here I've had to up my game, thanks very much. I made a delicious lasagne the other night, veggie mince of course. Even Holly ate it."

Julie let out a low whistle. "Bloody hell, it must have been good."

"It was." I pretended to preen. "We don't really need you here anymore, to be honest."

"So it seems."

There was a crash and a cry in the background. Julie

looked round. "Zinnie! What are you doing?"

"I was trying to get my flask down. You were too busy talking to Alice. I've got to get to school."

"Oops," I said, wondering when Zinnia had got so grown up – and so stroppy. "I'll let you go."

"Alright. Have fun at your mum and dad's. Tell them I wish I was there too."

"We all wish that. Love to Luke." I blew her a kiss and she vanished from the screen.

Now, I laugh as Mum puts a label on the mince pies – *Baked by Phil*. "Won't that put people off?"

"I heard that, Alice!" Dad appears behind me. "They'll be the first thing that goes, you wait and see."

"Sure. Well, good work, Dad. But just bear in mind, man cannot live on mince pies alone."

"He hasn't tried mine yet."

As the clock strikes one, the doorbell goes and there are Bea, David and Martin, along with Esme and Tyler. If I thought Zinnia was growing up, these two are something else. Proper teenagers, but that isn't the insult some people might assume. I smile at them and usher them in, and predictably Esme is immediately mobbed by Holly, while Ben tries to play it cool with Tyler though I can see he's desperate to hang out with him.

"If you guys want to use the attic rooms you're welcome to," I say. "Just go on up."

"Thanks Alice," smiles Esme.

"I'll call you when the buffet's open," I reassure them, leading the way up the stairs to the attic rooms, which Julie and I used to rent from David, a long time ago. What a strange turn of phrase that is, 'when the buffet's open'.

What does that actually mean to my children's generation? Will the humble buffet really become a thing of the past?

I don't know anyone of my age who does buffets, or has dinner parties for that matter, but I would put money on them provoking a real sense of nostalgia. I remember when Mum and Dad would either host or be invited to dinner parties almost every weekend, or so it seemed to me. That actually really could be a great little business, I think. I picture seventies-style crockery and serviettes folded into swans. Prawn cocktail for starters and a fondue for mains. Very *Abigail's Party* but hopefully not so dark. If Julie was here, I'd be pushing her to try it out. Then again, if Julie was here we'd still have our hands full with Amethi and another business idea would be the furthest thing from our minds.

Mum could do it, though. Sue's Soirees. *Bring back the buffet.* What would Dad do? I think of his pies. Phil's Pies. Perfect. Phil's Perfect Pies. I might be onto something. Then again, maybe I've just been working in PR too long – though it's only been a year.

With these thoughts in my mind, I trot back down the stairs, only to be met by David halfway up, on the mini-landing next to the stairwell window.

"Alice!" He hugs me. "How are you?"

"All the better for seeing you," I grin. "I miss you."

"I miss you too!" David got into a bit of trouble with his old law firm when he punched the father of one of Tyler's classmates. Nothing came of it but it provided David with a chance to rethink his life and he's begun work with a very small family law firm which is keeping him increasingly busy. "I thought when the kids got older we'd have more time to get our lives back," he says. "But actually if I'm not working I'm shipping them to parties or surf lessons or having their mates over…"

"They need you more than ever, I guess."

"I think they do. But I'm also very aware that we're heading into the last few years where they will really need us in the way they do." David looks wistfully out of the window. I follow his gaze and I'm pleased to see a small patch of blue in the sky. It must be the unrealistic optimist in me but even the slightest tint of colour breaking through the clouds can lift my spirits.

"It's a weird thought, isn't it? One minute they rely on you for absolutely everything – feeding, getting washed, tying shoelaces… and you wish they would hurry up and learn to do it themselves just so you might get a moment's rest – then all of a sudden they are doing it, and you realise you'll never have those times again."

"This is all sounding a bit morose." A voice comes from behind us.

"Martin!" I smile.

David's husband walks up the steps towards us, hugging me and then putting his arm round David. "If I'm not careful he'll be wanting another."

"You wouldn't… would you?"

"I would!" David says. "But Martin thinks two is good. And he's probably right."

"I'm definitely right," Martin says. "And I want me and you to have some time to do stuff too. Go travelling. Learn to sail–" David pulls a face at me and Martin gives him a stern look – "don't think I didn't see that, David. You'll love it if you give it a try."

"If you say so."

I see a large, bear-sized shape behind the glass of the

front door so I excuse myself, trotting down the stairs and across the floorboards to let the next guests in. "Craig!" I say, kissing him on the cheek. The petite Diane appears behind him. "And Diane! Thank you for coming."

"Thanks for inviting us. Well, thanks to Sue and Phil I suppose!" She smiles, her cheeks rosy against her soft pink pashmina, which is dotted with shiny raindrops.

"Come on in. Mum and Dad are in the lounge, I think."

I peer round the door and see Sam is in conversation with Peter Oswald, one of the former mayors. Sam shoots a look at me, which I correctly read as a plea for help. Peter is a lovely man but he definitely knows how to talk.

I sidle over. "Excuse me Peter, I'm sorry to interrupt but I could just do with a hand from Sam if you don't mind."

"Of course, of course," Peter says jovially. "When your good lady needs you, Sam…"

"Exactly. Duty calls," Sam offers a what-can-you-do type shrug and he follows me into the kitchen. We both start giggling. I feel like a teenager again, socialising with my parents' friends.

"Not interrupting something, are we?" David appears in the doorway, Martin grinning over his shoulder.

"No, I just had to rescue Sam from PO."

"Oh yes, good work Alice. Do you know, I feel positively young, mingling with this lot," says David.

"I know what you mean," I say. "It doesn't happen often these days."

"Should we sneak outside for a cigarette?" Martin asks.

"You wouldn't… you haven't, have you?" I am surprised, I thought Martin hated smoking.

"No! Anyway it's all about the vapes these days, didn't you know? Tell you what though, we could grab a bottle and head outside for a bit, couldn't we? Do you think your mum and dad would mind, Alice?"

I hear a peal of laughter from Mum in the front room. "No, I really don't think they would."

"Great. Get one of those bottles of champagne, David."

"But we bought them for Sue and Phil…"

"We brought two, didn't we? Come on, let's live a little! You're always saying we're too grown up these days."

David grabs a bottle from the fridge. Sam and I bring out two glasses each, and Martin leads the way into the garden.

"Isn't it your kids who are meant to be sneaking outside with a bottle?" Sam asks.

"Well yeah, but I don't think it would be champagne," says Martin. "Anyway, they're far too sensible. We're Gen X. This is what we do."

"I think you'll find Alice and I are Millennials," says Sam, mock-superiorly.

"Well you can't have everything," says David, popping the bottle.

I'm gratified to see that the blue patch of sky has widened and I hope it will soon have stretched itself all the way above us. The gulls are making the most of the improvement in the weather, soaring high above us and out over the rooftops. It could almost feel like spring is upon us but one look at David and Martin, resplendent in penguin and snowman jumpers, and I quickly remember we are actually well into December.

The garden benches are wet so we have to stand, but it all adds to that illicit feeling. Here we are, stuck somewhere in between our kids upstairs and the adults in the front room. I mean, we are adults too, officially. It just doesn't always feel like it. Maybe it never does, for anyone.

The bubbles go quickly to my head and David pours me a second glass. I look at Sam. "I'll drive," he says. "Or we could stay here, if your mum and dad don't mind. We could both have a drink…"

"Go on!" Martin says. "We're staying at Bea's. We could make a night of it. Go clubbing…"

"I think you're getting a bit ahead of yourself now, my love," says David. "You know perfectly well you'll be snoring on the sofa by half nine."

"A man can dream, can't he?"

It feels good, being here with my husband and my friends. We've known each other a long time now. And while they may not be Julie, each one of these men is extremely important to me. By the time we head back indoors, my cheeks are aching from laughing.

"Buffet time!" says Mum, who I think may also have had a glass or two.

"Bring back the buffet!" I say.

"What?"

"Oh, nothing. I'll call the kids down."

"Lovely."

Almost before I have finished my sentence, the four children come galloping down the stairs.

"Here come the gannets," says Dad.

Tyler proves Dad right, piling his plate high, only stopping when Martin warningly says, "Ty…"

I can see Ben is planning to do the same but I know full well he'll leave half of it.

"Just come back for more if you're hungry," I say, and he looks at me resentfully, which makes Martin laugh.

Dad comes round topping up everyone's glasses and the four of us 'young'uns' take our plates into the kitchen, leaning against the worktops while we eat. Then it's time for Dad's mince pies (about which we all make sure we compliment him generously), and then party games.

"Will Ben and Holly play?" Dad asks.

"I don't know. I think they're happy as they are." I've been up to check on them all and as I'd suspected, the TV is on – CBBC, I'm pleased to see, Esme and Tyler realising that there is a level of suitability for my two – and Tyler and Esme are on their phones, Ben gazing wistfully at them.

"I'm getting a phone for Christmas," I heard him say as I was heading back downstairs.

Not this Christmas, I think, smiling. *And not for many more to come if I have my way.* I am quite sure that when it comes to the magic of Christmas morning all thoughts of a phone will be forgotten.

We play charades and then Peter suggests sardines, but I am glad that Mum vetoes this, instead bringing out a flip chart. "*Win, Lose or Draw!*" she says.

"I remember that show!" Martin says approvingly.

"And *Give us a Clue!*" says Bea.

"Yes, they don't make them like that anymore," says Peter Oswald's wife, Samantha.

"Remember *Blankety Blank*?"

"Isn't that still on?"

For a while the room is abuzz with nostalgic talk, until Dad has had enough. "Come on!" he says. "Let's play."

He is first to draw, and getting increasingly frustrated at his team's inability to make sense of his scribbles, which look to me like a child's drawing of a pair of breasts, when the doorbell goes. "Who's that?" Dad asks.

"I don't know! Everyone's here, aren't they?" asks Mum.

"I'll go," I offer. "I'm not in this round."

"Oh would you, love? Thank you."

"No problem."

The incoming night has slowly started to suck away at the day and the hallway is in near-darkness so I switch on the light. "Just coming!" I say, expecting it to be a delivery driver. Instead, I open the door to somebody who looks familiar but who I can't immediately place.

"Alice?" he asks. "But look at you, all grown up."

This is a bit creepy. The man is in semi-darkness while I am standing fully in the light. I try to peer at him without appearing drunk or rude. I don't know if I quite manage.

"It's me. Nigel."

I still don't know him.

"Nigel. Simpkins. From back home."

"Nigel?" I say, and it all comes flooding back. He was a work colleague of Dad's. A single man, and a regular visitor to our house, sometimes to those dinner parties I mentioned earlier but more often than not he'd come round alone, for an evening after work. And he'd always come to see us on Christmas Eve. I remember it well now, how he'd bring us presents and mine would normally be a frilly dress or a book far too young for me but I'd have to say thank you graciously and Mum would do the same with her apron, or tomato-slicer, or other thoughtful woman-type-gift. But he was not a bad person at all. I just don't think he knew many children. Or women.

He looks old now and not as tall as I recall, and his coat seems to hang off him, as if he's bought one to grow into. Maybe he's lost some height and weight, or perhaps it's just because I'm an adult now too. He's balding, and what hair he has is white, as opposed to the gingery-brown I remember, but I can see clearly that it's him.

"Come in!" I say, finally summoning my manners but wondering what to do as we are clearly in the middle of a party. Mum and Dad weren't expecting him, were they?

"Nigel?" Mum says behind me. From the expression on her face I see that no, she clearly wasn't expecting him at all.

"Hello Sue. Is this a bad time?" He looks crestfallen.

"No, no, of course not. We're – we've got a few friends round, for a little get together, but you're very welcome to join us. My goodness, wait till Phil sees you!"

I take Nigel's oversized coat and Mum ushers him through to the lounge, where I hear Dad greet him warmly and the other guests immediately make him feel at home.

Another blast from the past. What a strange day this is turning out to be, but it all feels good. I sit on the arm of the settee, while Sam gets a drink for Nigel, who is pulled straight into the game – a willing participant in our team as Karen stands up to draw what turns out to be her depiction of the Queen song *Big Bottomed Girls*. The less said about that, the better.

5

By five o'clock, Martin and Peter Oswald are both asleep on the settee, Peter's head lolling occasionally towards Martin's shoulder before jerking upright again. For his part, Martin has a shiny trail of drool tracking the way down his chin. Of course we have all taken lots of photos, and Dad has been trying unsuccessfully to balance Christmas cracker hats on their heads, to much quiet sniggering from the rest of us.

"To think Martin was on about going clubbing!" David laughs. "I suppose it was nice that he thought he could."

"It's quite sweet really," says Samantha Oswald. "And has anyone noticed it's a lot quieter here now my husband's asleep?"

We mutter and laugh politely, none of us feeling quite able to agree with Peter's wife. It's fine for her to joke about him but I feel like she's the type of person who might change their tune any minute and take offence if any of us did the same.

"Some people say *I* talk too much," Nigel offers.

"No!" says Mum, putting her arm through his. "I don't believe it."

I look from her to him, and see her affectionate sarcasm has gone over his head. Nigel just looks pleasantly relaxed.

"Honestly," he says. "They used to say it at the office. Didn't they, Phil?"

"I can't say I noticed," Dad says politely.

"Oh they did. And when I'm at work if I pop into the office they call me Nattering Nigel."

Dad and Nigel both retired at a similar time but, while Dad has found many ways to keep himself occupied, and taken delight in having so much time for gardening, it seems that retirement didn't agree with Nigel. He has told me at great lengths how he is now a Sainsbury's delivery driver. "And before that, I was a Tesco delivery driver, and before that Asda. I'm like Goldilocks – the third one is just right." I have heard him use this line with Mum too, and with Ron, who is thankfully a lot more polite than Karen. Sam's mum makes me laugh, with her unwillingness to suffer fools gladly or otherwise. Not that I am calling Nigel a fool but let's just say she hasn't got much patience with people like him.

And Nigel is actually a very nice man. I remember that from his visits to us during our childhood. There was nothing intimidating about him, like there could be with some of my parents' other friends, but I suppose I thought he was just a bit… boring. Mum and Dad had taken him under their wing when he'd moved to the area, having recently split up with his wife and got a new job at the place where Dad worked.

I think that's something else that's different now. Work colleagues are more disconnected. I suppose that, like me, lots of people work from home, and technology has enabled teams to spring up remotely, but it seems to me that places of work used to have more of a family feel. It's a long time for me now since I worked at World of Stationery, but even then it wasn't like it was for Mum and Dad. I did like the people I worked with and by and large we got on well as a team, but I can't imagine any of us inviting a new colleague round for dinner just because it seemed like a nice thing to do. They would be included on a night out – of course – but there is something very personal about inviting somebody into your home and I think a lot of us shy away from that kind of thing nowadays. In a way it's not a bad thing. We all need our space, and lives away from the workplace. And maybe with colleagues becoming less like family, people's actual families can take more of a prominent place in their lives.

Luckily for me it is not an issue. It's just me and Shona, and we already know each other. But Sam works in a larger place, with people from all over the south-west. What would I think if he told me he'd invited one of them round for dinner – and what if he expected me to cook for them? It seems such an alien concept. He'd never do that without asking, but I'm sure it's how things used to be. It does feel like we are much more keen to protect our privacy these days and perhaps less willing to let strangers in, to our homes or our lives.

As Martin and Peter snore on, the rest of us move through to the dining room and Mum makes some coffee. In all honesty, I could happily curl up on the sofa on the other side of Martin and have a little doze myself. I am sure I'm not the only one.

Dad suggests Christmas carols, but I think we are all partied out.

"It's only 6pm!" Dad protests but it feels more like midnight. Sam takes coffees to Peter and Martin, who eventually make their sheepish way through to join us and it's not long before the guests begin to take their leave. Dad and Mum both look tired out.

"The cruise will do you the world of good," I say.

"Oh, are you going away?" asks Nigel, who has not yet had enough.

"Yes, we're cruising for Christmas!" Mum laughs at her alliteration.

"Oh, really?" There is evident disappointment in Nigel's face and his voice.

"Yes, and we can't wait!" says Dad, not always the brightest when it comes to picking up on other people's moods.

"What are your plans, Nigel?" Mum asks carefully.

"Well I had been going to ask if you'd like to join me for dinner, at that hotel in the town. The Bay, is it? I know it's last minute, and of course you've got family. It was a stupid idea, sorry."

"No, it's a lovely idea," Mum says. "And we'd have loved to. Although to be honest if we were here we probably would be spending the day with Alice, Sam and the kids."

"Are you staying here, Alice?" Nigel's face brightens a little.

"Yes, we are. We're having our first family Christmas, just the four of us." I answer hurriedly, keen to let him know we have plans just in case he invites us for dinner. I don't fancy spending Christmas Day with somebody we barely know. But maybe I'm being presumptuous thinking he'd want to spend it with us.

"That sounds nice," he says. "What an idiot I am. I should have checked with you first Phil, I am stupid."

"No you're not!" Dad says, finally stepping in to comfort his old friend and colleague. "We're really pleased to see you. I'm just sorry we didn't know you were coming, we could have invited you to stay here."

I glance at Mum to see her smile drop slightly.

"But Sam and Alice and the kids are staying here tonight," Dad continues and Mum's relief is almost palpable, "and tomorrow we're going to be finishing our packing. Where are you staying? The Bay?"

"Ah no, I'm actually on tour, Phil. In this little beauty…" Nigel plucks his phone from his pocket and unlocks it then shows it to Dad.

"Hey, that's a nice van you've got there!" Dad looks genuinely impressed.

Nigel shows his phone to us all, displaying a picture of him standing in front of an expensive-looking motorhome.

"That looks great!" I say.

"I'll show you round it if you like. I've parked it down by the Island, is it? I know you're not meant to stay overnight but I thought it wouldn't hurt…"

"You might just get away with it at this time of year," Dad says, "but as a local councillor I shouldn't be telling you that."

"Are you, a councillor, Phil?" Nigel looks impressed.

"For my sins," Dad says, looking a bit smug.

"So do you want to come and see her? Bertha, I call her. Big Bertha."

Mum and I look at each other. Sam, I notice, has made himself scarce and by the sound of things is currently washing up mugs in the kitchen. I glance out of the back

38

door into the quiet darkness of the garden. I'm quite happy staying put in Mum and Dad's lovely warm house.

"I think Alice will need to sort Ben and Holly out," says Dad, once more stepping into the breach. "And Sue's going to have a lot of tidying up to do. You know." Normally Mum would jump to her own defence at such a line but she knows Dad's just helping to get her off the hook.

"Ah yes, you did always keep a lovely house, Sue," says Nigel, almost wistfully. "I always felt at home when I came to visit."

"That's lovely of you, Nigel. Thank you. I would love to see your van but maybe during the daytime would be better."

"Of course. Stupid of me again. Honestly, I don't know what I was thinking. I just had this idea of turning up unannounced and surprising you all."

"You did do that, Nigel."

"Yes Sue, but I didn't know you were having a party. Or that you were going away."

"Come on Nige," Dad says kindly. "I'd love to see your van."

"Really?"

"Of course."

"Even though it's dark?"

"Yes. And I can take you for a pint too, before we retire for the night."

"That sounds smashing."

So Dad and Nigel get their coats and head out into the night but not before Mum has pulled Dad back and kissed him.

"What was that for?" he asks, looking pleased.

"You know what."

We wait a few moments after the front door has closed then sigh in relief.

"Has he gone?" Sam asks, coming into the hallway.

"Yes, no thanks to you!" I say. "Ah, but poor Nigel. He's a nice man."

"He is," says Mum. "But fancy just turning up like that! And thinking we'd just be free to come out for Christmas dinner. He knows we've got family."

"But he hasn't," says Sam. "Has he?"

"No," I admit.

"Poor guy."

"You've changed your tune. Maybe you should have gone with Dad to see Nigel's van."

"Big Bertha," Mum reminds me.

"That's right. She's a real beauty," I say in a poor imitation of Nigel.

"I do like a good van," muses Sam. "And the freedom of the open road…"

"It's starting to appeal to you, is it? The bachelor lifestyle?"

"Well…"

"Count your blessings!" I say, hitting him on the arm.

"I do. Every day. And speaking of blessings, hadn't we better call our little angels down to get some tea?"

"Yes," I say, "we really had. I'll go and see what they're up to."

"I'll put the oven on," says Mum.

"And I'll check the fire," offers Sam. "And I'll just see if there's a splash more wine..." He picks up a bottle of red from the table and pours what's left into his glass.

"You go and sit down, Sam," says Mum. "You've been working hard."

So have I! I want to protest but I stop myself. It's my

inbuilt reaction and I know it's just childish really. Instead, I say, "You go and sit down too, Mum. You've been on your feet all day. I'll put the oven on then I'll go and get Ben and Holly. No, don't say anything. Go and sit down and put your feet up."

"That's me told," says Mum.

"Yes, it is."

As I go through to the kitchen, I hear Mum and Sam chatting and feel a little flood of warmth at how well they get on. I don't need to jump down her throat, as I nearly had. She was just being Mum, and being kind to her son-in-law. It doesn't mean she doesn't think I work hard. Sometimes I have to remind myself that I may be her and dad's daughter but I am no longer an actual child.

Speaking of children, when I go upstairs I stop outside the door of what was Julie's room, a long time ago, and which is now a little sitting room for any guests who come to stay with Mum and Dad. It sounds like the TV is on still, but I can't hear any voices. I push the door open gently and see Ben and Holly in a little re-enactment of Martin and Peter, Holly's head resting on Ben's shoulder and both of them asleep with their mouths open, breathing softly.

I cannot think of a better expression than to say that my heart melts. I pull my phone from my pocket and then I think better of it. I don't need to photograph everything, and besides... oh sod it. *Click.* This is too cute not to show Sam at least.

I think for a moment what to do. Leave them sleeping? Cover them with a duvet? But there's no way they'll sleep through the night like this, and they will need some food or they'll get to 2am and be ravenous.

I kneel down in front of them and kiss first Holly and then Ben on their soft, warm cheeks.

"Wake up, sleepyheads."

Just waking up, Ben is less keen to be cool and he's cuddly like he's always been. I have to appreciate these moments. He wraps his arms round my neck and pushes his face against me. Holly, meanwhile, tries her best to sleep on, pushing her thumb into her mouth and screwing her eyes tightly shut.

"Come on, you two," I say, sitting down between them, then pulling them both onto my lap. "Have a few moments to wake up then we'll go and get some tea."

"Too tired," Holly says.

"It's pizza."

"OK." She is suddenly more awake.

Nevertheless, both are content to sit and cuddle just a little while longer and I watch the TV, without taking in whatever programme is on, too busy thinking about how lucky I am having my children in my life. Nigel crosses my mind and my heart squeezes in sympathy for him.

"What's wrong, Mummy?" Ben asks.

"Nothing, why?"

"You just did a big sigh. Didn't she, Holly?"

"Yes," Holly says adamantly but she'll agree with almost anything Ben says.

"Oh, it was a happy sigh. Being here with you two."

They both hug me tighter, and then put their arms around each other as well. I close my eyes and, as I often do in these situations, remember Lizzie. Friend, colleague, yoga instructor, unapologetic hippy. Another great person I'm missing – she is somewhere in Northern Italy at the moment with her partner Med and their van – but I know what she'd tell me. *Don't think about what's not. Try and appreciate everything you've got.* I hold my children to me and hear Lizzie's voice in my mind. *Breathe, Alice. Be in the moment, and just breathe.*

6

The next day, we are all exhausted. Mum and Dad make us breakfast and Dad tells us about his unplanned evening out with Nigel. He had phoned Mum to say that he was staying out a bit longer and he still wasn't back by the time we'd gone to bed. Having said that, I bet it wasn't much after half past nine and I fell asleep pretty much straightaway so it's not all that surprising that I didn't hear him come in.

"I was back by ten," he tells us, and checks Ben and Holly are out of earshot. They've wolfed their breakfasts down and are in the lounge watching *The Zoo* on CBBC. Dad continues. "Poor bloke."

"Nigel?" I ask, though who else would he be talking about?

"Yeah, I think he's just really lonely."

"Ah it's a shame," says Mum.

"He's a nice man," I observe and, wanting to lighten the mood, "Still very chatty."

"Lonely people often are," Mum says, and I feel chastened. "Do you remember our neighbour, Mrs Todd? Back home? You couldn't get away from her. I remember trying to hurry past her house sometimes, if I was in a hurry, but she'd always seem to spot me or already be on her doorstep, like she was just waiting for somebody to pass by. She probably was. She'd been on her own for years. Her husband died a long time before we moved in."

"She had children, didn't she? Or a son, at least?" I ask, dimly remembering our old neighbour.

"Yes, she did, but he lived a long way from her. She did used to go up to him for Christmas and New Year, I remember he'd come and collect her, and I remember how excited she was leading up to it. She'd start preparing for Christmas in September. It gave her something to look forward to, and something to do. She was always very good to you too. Bags of sweets on Hallowe'en, toffee apples for bonfire night, and she always gave us a tin of Quality Street for Christmas."

"What happened to her?"

"She went up to live near her son in the end. I think she was in sheltered accommodation of some kind. She did write, and send cards. I think she liked it there. I suppose she had more people around her, and it meant her son could get to see her more easily too."

"Couldn't she have gone to live with him?" Sam asks.

"I don't know," says Mum. "It's not always that easy."

"Would you want your mum to live with us?" I ask, the words out of my mouth before I've had a chance to think them through.

"God no!" Sam laughs then looks shame-faced. "But she could, of course, if she needed to. I mean, if it was OK with you…"

Mum just smiles. "See, it's not that easy, is it? People have got busy lives. And us oldies don't want to hold our children back. Or get in the way. Be a burden… Anyway, sorry love, tell us about Nigel!" She looks at Dad.

"Oh, I'm allowed to talk again, am I?" he says. "I think your mum's right though, Alice. Nigel is just a very lonely man. I think he always was. That's why we used to have him round to ours, isn't it love?" Mum nods in confirmation. "That's not to say we didn't like him on his own merits, but you know, we don't necessarily have a lot in common. I remember when he started in the office though, and he'd had a horrible break-up with his wife. She'd left him for somebody else. I found him in tears in the gents one day, and he told me all about it. Poor bloke. I invited him round, there and then. I knew your mum wouldn't mind. And he came over, and your mum did him some tea, and he played with you and your dolls house for hours. You wouldn't leave him alone!"

"Really?" I don't remember this.

"Yes!" Mum laughs. "I suppose maybe you were lonely in your own way. You didn't have a brother or sister, and so any unsuspecting visitor, young or old, became the sole object of your attention."

I feel my cheeks flush a little, even though this is child-me we are talking about.

"It was sweet!" Mum says. "You were sweet. I don't think anyone minded. And I do remember Nigel taking a real interest in you, in the nicest way. You'd bring him a pile of books to read to you and he happily would. You used to sit on the arm of the chair and hand him book after book."

"After book!" adds Dad.

"Oh my god, I was a real attention-seeker!"

"Still are," mutters Sam, and I nudge him.

I think back. Maybe I do remember Nigel reading to me. But it's a long time ago. A lot of my memories are hazy and I'm not always sure if they're real, or imagined and based on what somebody else told me happened. Either way, I feel bad for him now.

"He must think a lot of you two, to come all this way. And to have thought he'd take you out for Christmas dinner!" I picture his delight at this brilliant idea of his, and how he might have imagined Mum and Dad's reaction. Ah, it makes me sad.

"I know," Mum says. "It was a lovely thought, too. I suppose if he doesn't have family of his own, he maybe doesn't realise how busy Christmas is, and how people make plans so far in advance."

"So is he staying on in town?" I ask. "I don't think he'll be very popular if he camps out in the car park for much longer."

"No, he said he's going to move on today. He's got a niece or something in Devon so he's going to travel up to see her."

"That's nice. But I hope he gives her plenty of notice."

"I did try to gently suggest that. Anyway, it was nice to see the man and have a couple of pints with him, though I'm suffering for it," Dad says, rubbing his head. "It's an afternoon nap for me today."

"And every day," says Mum, ruffling his hair fondly then resting her hand on his.

"True, true."

When we head home, I ask Sam to drive past the Island car park. If Nigel is still there I'd like to wish him a happy Christmas, but his van has already gone. Dad said he'd invited Nigel to come back down when the weather's warmer, so hopefully I'll get a chance to see him then. I will be a better person next year, I tell myself. I will stop looking inwards so much and try to put myself out for other people more. Natalie springs to mind and I think she would not be a bad place to start. I did message her to say that I'd managed to double-book this weekend, but she hasn't replied, although I could see she's read my message. At first I didn't give it a second thought, but yesterday morning I popped round, just to apologise, but there was no answer and the house was quiet. Rob's car wasn't on the drive so I guess they'd maybe all gone out together.

"Shall we stop?" I ask Sam. "Park up?" The sea beyond the car park is glossy and glistening; an exquisite peacock-blue today. "Just to blow the cobwebs away?"

He looks at me. "Why not?"

"Don't want to!" says Holly.

"Come on Hols, we'll go up the scramble way," Sam says. "I'll race you."

"I'll win!" she says delightedly. Sam definitely knows how to win his daughter round.

He pulls the car into a space by the grass and we clamber out.

"I wish Meg was here," I say to Sam.

"I know. Me too. Mum said she didn't even want to go for a wee when she went to let her out this morning," he says quietly.

"Oh god. I don't even want to think about it."

"I know."

Ron was a vet before he retired and it was thanks to him that we got to keep Meg; she belonged to a client of his who couldn't look after her any longer. It's so good that he can keep an eye on her now, as she grows older. We can't pretend it's not happening, and we don't even know what age she is. I can't bear to think of her not being around anymore, or how the kids will deal with it, but I know we will have to face up to it one of these days.

I shake the thought from my head. *Be in the moment.* The wind is strong across this open stretch of land which juts boldly out into the sea. Holly's hair is blowing into her face. I tuck it back behind her ears and whisper to her. She grins. Sam is pointing out a bird to Ben. I seize the chance, taking Holly's hand.

"Race you!" I shout. Holly laughs with glee. We run, me and my little girl, up the slope, Sam and Ben hot on our heels as soon as they realise what's going on.

"Come on Holly," I say, already breathless as I give her a leg up and through the little rocky crevice, then I crawl and climb up myself, scraping my knees slightly through my jeans but not caring. Holly is already racing up the grass towards the chapel and I'm not far behind but then Ben passes me, laughing and nearly but not quite reaching his sister, who arrives at the chapel and tears up the steps, touching the timeless stone walls. Ben is moments behind. I wonder if he deliberately allowed her to win. No, I think. He's good but he's not that good.

I feel a tug on my coat, and Sam is swinging me round.

"Hey!" I laugh.

He catches me around my waist. "Hey yourself! Cheat!"

"You snooze, you lose," I say, looking into his laughing eyes. He kisses me, and pulls me to him, and I feel the comfort of being with this man so familiar to me. His shape, his strength, his smell, his breath. To know somebody this well, it's a privilege. I may lament the passing of the early days of excitement and romance but would I swap this to have them again? Well yes maybe I would sometimes, but I know the value of this. What we have is special. And there are people like Nigel, who have never known it, and almost certainly never will. *Appreciate everything you've got.* I hear those words again and I smile as I hold my cheek against Sam's chest, listening to his heart beating, still fast from the sudden rush up the Island.

Thank you, Lizzie, I think, and imagine her so many miles away, across the sea and deep into southern Europe, somehow hearing those words... knowing her, she probably can. I take Sam's hand and we walk up towards our children, then all four of us stand at the low-level wall, Sam and I holding our children safely to us while we look down over the tussocks of grass and rocky outcrops to the waves crashing far below.

7

Back home, Ben and Holly are quite happy to settle down on the sofa, one either side of Sam. I switch the Christmas tree lights on and stand back, thinking of that year when I was pregnant with Holly and the lights seemed to have a life of their own. Could we really have had an actual spirit with us then? The more time that passes by, the less convinced I am that I didn't just imagine the whole thing, my hormones playing havoc with me and Lizzie's story about poor Elizabeth Grayley and baby Rose seeping into my consciousness. Maybe one night I should visit that cove again, where Elizabeth is said to haunt the sands, see if she is still there. I never would, of course. Not on my own at least. I'm far too much of a wimp.

What I will do though is go and see Natalie. When Mum was talking about our old neighbour Mrs Todd, and how she used to sometimes hurry past Mrs Todd's house to avoid being caught up in conversation, it did provoke a little twinge of guilt in me because I know I do that to Natalie sometimes.

"I'm just going down the road," I say to Sam. "I'll drop off our neighbourly Christmas cards."

"Alright," he says, his head resting against Ben's. They both look worn out, and so does Holly. Why do we do this to ourselves, I wonder… just for the sake of one day. I am increasingly coming to see it's not really about just one day. Christmas has become about so much more and the many celebrations might on the one hand distract us from the dark nights and mornings but on the other serve to create more things we have to remember and plan for (and find the money for) in our already-busy lives.

I grab my keys and my coat and the small pile of cards from the shelf near the door then step out into the street. Darkness is already wrapping itself around the afternoon, but all along the street there are twinkly lights creating a warming, festive glow. Jill and Raymond, who live next to Natalie, have a pair of light-up reindeer grazing on their lawn while two doors further on an inflatable Father Christmas tries unrelentingly but with no success to climb onto the roof above the front door. There are strings of twinkling icicles suspended below gutters, and trees and bushes dotted with multi-coloured lights, making the onset of darkness feel cosy and welcoming.

Natalie's house stands out as one of the few that doesn't bear any sign of Christmas, outwardly at least. It surprises me as Natalie strikes me as one of those people who might love to decorate, and celebrate, but at Halloween it was the same. She said Rob didn't really approve of Halloween, which is fair enough. But does he also disapprove of Christmas? Even Sam – always favouring the 'less is more' approach – has agreed to have a shooting star lighting up the wall near our front door. And I sneakily got some solar lights for our flower beds, which Ben and Holly and I put in place before he got back from work one night.

I can see the curtains are already drawn and Rob's car is again not on the drive so possibly they are all still out or maybe he has already left on another work trip. I don't know why they moved to Cornwall to be honest, he is away so much, and it's not exactly convenient here for getting anywhere except the rest of Cornwall. I know that Natalie doesn't drive so I imagine that Lincolnshire, where her mum is, must feel a world away.

I ring the doorbell, checking my phone as well to see if Natalie has responded to the WhatsApp I sent on Friday.

Hi Natalie. I am so sorry about this. I know I suggested we do something tomorrow but I had totally forgotten it's my parents' Christmas party. I am a total idiot. Can we rearrange? X

I thought that sounded OK – I didn't want to give too long an explanation in case it sounded like I was trying too hard to make up an excuse. But maybe that's my own inner guilt. I can see from the two blue ticks that she's read the message so it's a bit weird she hasn't replied. But perhaps she was busy doing something else when she read it and just forgot. It's quite possible I am not as important to Natalie's life as I seem to think sometimes. I'm sure she has other things going on and hopefully other – better – friends around here.

Nobody answers the door and the house remains quiet. It's quite possible they have all gone away for the weekend, of course. Maybe they are visiting family; perhaps Natalie herself had other plans she'd forgotten about when I suggested getting together.

I push the Christmas card through the letterbox then I continue down the road, posting a card for each of the neighbours along the way. It's a nice street, I'm glad to be here. It may not be Amethi but this feels right for this stage in our lives. There are lots of families and friends for our children, and across the road it's just trees and a road and then countryside so we're really lucky, it's very quiet.

As if to remind me of this, as I wander back home an owl hoots from somewhere in the trees over the way. Then, as I go back past Natalie's house my attention is caught by what I think is a movement at one of the upstairs windows but I turn and see there is nothing there. My mind goes back to the story of Elizabeth and Rose and the Christmas when Holly was born. Is there a ghost in Natalie's house? It seems unlikely. Still, I pull my coat around myself and walk just a little more quickly.

***

It's bath night for Ben and Holly, and an early night for all of us, though the children find it hard to wind down.

Ben prefers to bath alone these days, which Holly is struggling with, and she keeps trying to come into the bathroom.

"Holl-ee!" Ben says. "Get out. I need my privacy."

"But Mummy's in there."

"Yeah, well…" Ben struggles to rationalise this. "She's Mummy."

That much is true. "Go on downstairs, Holly. Ask Daddy to dry your hair for you."

I peer out of the door to see my little girl, cosy in pink pyjamas and snuggly white dressing gown, clutching her cuddly dog toy, reluctantly go downstairs. "Daddy!" she calls. "Can you dry my hair?"

"Of course. Come on in here, and shut the door, let's keep the room nice and warm, shall we?"

I turn back to Ben. "Are you all set for tomorrow?"

Tomorrow is the dress rehearsal in front of the whole school. His role as a Roman soldier doesn't feel very Christmassy somehow, but he's leading his troops in a search for Mary and Joseph, who have tucked themselves safely away in the stable of the inn. Ben loves his part though, and has learned his lines well. As have we all, the number of times we have heard them.

"I think so," he says, suddenly doubtful.

"You'll be great," I tell him. "I can't wait to see it on Tuesday. And Granny Karen and Ron will be there."

"They won't be at the front, will they?"

I have had to have a quiet word with Karen, who has previously insisted on getting to school plays and assemblies early, placing coats and cardigans on chairs to save them for me and Sam, and Mum and Dad. Holly loves to see us all there but Ben is not so keen and I'm not sure many of the other parents are very impressed either.

"No, they won't. The seats are numbered this time, so I got four in the third row back."

"OK." I notice he has vague shadows under his eyes. Maybe it was too much, going to Mum and Dad's and staying up late when he's got so much going on at school too. But we just get carried along on the wave of Christmas, from parties to carol services to discos to plays, to pantomimes and family get-togethers, pub lunches, all the while present-swapping and hugging and kissing and laughing, and missing those no longer here… No wonder the children are tired out. No wonder we all are. But maybe that is what helps to make Christmas Day – and to my mind even more so Boxing Day – so sweet. Finally we can stop, and step back from the world. Retreat into the hearts of our families, at least those of us lucky enough to have them.

"Hey, it's going to be loads of fun," I tell him. "And then it's just another day to go until the holidays. And it's the disco on the last day of term as well. All you'll be doing is watching Christmas films, messing about with your friends, and having fun."

Memories of my own school Christmases fill my mind; it's all still so vivid. The thrill of being in the classroom after the end of the school day, getting into our costumes under the glare of the strip lighting while the windows steamed up against the dark and cold outside. Knowing that parents, grandparents, friends' parents, were all sitting in the hall, waiting.

The novel sight of a Christmas tree in the school, and the over-excitement of the disco, dressed in our own clothes, nobody really dancing but boys skidding along the shiny floor on their knees. Teachers smiling and laughing with each other, looking forward to their own Christmases too.

"It's tiring, being a child," I say to Ben now. "For lots of good reasons, but there's always something going on. Something new to learn. It'll be good for you to have a rest over Christmas."

I know full well that until the big day has come and gone, there will be no resting. It's impossible. The anticipation is overwhelming. Maybe this year having a small Christmas, just the five of us, is exactly what we need.

***

I try to read a few pages of my book before I go to sleep. Sam has just got under the duvet, kissed me, turned over, and is already softly snoring, and my eyes are flickering; my mind too – going into strange thoughts and a semi-dreamlike state. I give in, marking my page and turning the light out then burrowing down under the covers and wrapping myself around Sam's back. I lay my head against his shoulder and enjoy the peace, and the softness of our darkened room. *Our space*, I think. *Mine and Sam's*. I smile to myself as I drift off.

But then I am wide awake, and startled. Somebody is banging something outside. I hear an angry shout.

"Sam?" I whisper. Nothing. Gently, I lift the cover away from me and tiptoe to the window. It's probably just somebody who's had a few too many drinks and been overwhelmed by a not-so-Christmassy spirit.

Along the road, most of the Christmas lights are still on and it takes me a moment to see past them and identify a vaguely familiar figure a few houses along, standing on the pavement and staring at his house.

It's Rob. What's he doing?

"Natalie!" he shouts. "Let me in."

Oh dear. This doesn't look good. I feel bad, spectating what is a private argument. Except Rob's made it everyone's business, standing out on the street like that. I am sure I won't be the only person keeping an eye on proceedings.

"You stupid bitch!" he shouts, and it touches something very deep within me, disturbing memories I would rather leave buried.

"Sam," I say and then, more loudly, I hiss, "Sam!"

He has a sudden, sharp intake of breath and sits up.

"What? What's up? Is Holly OK?"

That's it – our first reaction these days, even if we're half asleep. There's a little part of both of us that goes straight to Holly, and particularly overnight, when it's possible something might go wrong with her pump, or the cannula and tubing which constantly feed her little body insulin while we sleep.

"It's not Holly," I say, though now I want to check the app on my phone. "It's Rob. And Natalie."

"What?"

"Well it's Rob at least. He's out on the street shouting at her. He just called her a bitch."

"Where is she?"

"Not out there, as far as I can see. No, she can't be, he's shouted at her to let him in."

Sam joins me, putting a warm arm around my shoulder and peering through the curtains. Rob must know that he'll be being watched but maybe he is past the point of caring. He does seem very worked up. He kicks one of the reindeer, then hops as though he's hurt his foot. It would be comical, if it wasn't also so unpleasant.

"Raymond won't be pleased if he's seen that," observes Sam. He steps away from the window and starts rooting around in the clothes basket. "I'm going out there."

"You can't."

"I can."

"But it's… it's not any of our business."

"He's making it our business, Alice. And it's going to wake the kids. And what about his own two?"

"Yes, but…"

"Look, I'll just go and see what's going on, OK? Maybe having somebody else there will make him see sense."

I'm not convinced but I also think of Natalie, and Bobby and Courtney. If those children are awake this will be horrible for them.

"OK," I concede. "But if he gets nasty just come back home, alright?"

"If he gets nasty, call the police," Sam says.

"Do you think it will come to that?"

"Who knows?" Sam says grimly.

I get my phone from the charger and I take the chance to look at Holly's blood sugars but they're a lovely steady 6.4 so that's a comfort at least.

I also check WhatsApp. Still no reply from Natalie. Should I message her? Check she's OK? I don't know. There is a little reserved British part of me that thinks I shouldn't interfere.

But Geoff, I think, allowing myself to remember my boyfriend of long ago. Controlling, bordering on abusive, he was a charming man to begin with and he came into my life when I was reeling from what I perceived as Sam having just given me the cold shoulder. I was young, naïve and heartbroken. I was just what Geoff was looking for.

Natalie, I send, **are you OK?**

It takes a moment but then my message has been read and 'Natalie is typing…' I see, but no resulting message appears.

I look out of the window to see my lovely Sam is in conversation with Rob, who appears to be a bit calmer now. Sam puts a hand on his arm but Rob shrugs it off and Sam steps back ever so slightly. I can't hear what he's saying but suddenly Rob lunges towards him, grabs his collar and punches him.

"Shit!" I shout, dropping my phone and running downstairs without a second thought. I slip my feet into a pair of Sam's shoes, which are far too big for me, open the door, and run outside.

"Sam!" I shout. He is already walking towards me.

"Go back in, Alice," he says. "Bloke's a total prick."

I rarely see Sam angry but right now he's fuming. He is also, I see as he gets closer to the light, bleeding from his nose.

"Oh my god, are you OK? Where is he?" I look down the street, wanting to run at Rob and hit him back, though I already know I would never dare.

"He's gone," Sam says.

"Where to?"

"Fuck knows. He got in his car and drove off, straight after he hit me. He's probably had a skinful as well. I'm phoning the police. Hopefully he'll get pulled over and breathalysed."

"Let's see to your face first," I say, gently leading him inside. I am suddenly aware I'm outside on a cold December night in just my pyjamas and an oversized pair of trainers. I'm shivering and Sam is too. "Come on."

Even Meg has got up to see what's going on and she looks at Sam, her gentle eyes on him.

"It's OK girl," he says, stroking the side of her face.

I grab a towel from the downstairs toilet and hand it to Sam.

"For the blood," I say.

He looks down to see drops of red on his hoodie and on the floor.

"Don't worry about any of that, it's fine. Let's just get you sorted."

"Call the police, Alice," he says grimly. "Please. I'll tell you his registration plate."

"Alright. You just sit down and put your head forward. Pinch your nose... you know what to do." We are both trained first aiders. "What about Natalie though?" I ask. "She's at home?"

"He said so. Said she's chucked him out. Locked him out, too."

"Oh my god."

"Yeah."

"Why?"

"Don't know. He just said something about her being a stupid bitch."

The words send a chill through me but my emergency call is answered so I tell the call handler what's happened and relay Rob's registration plate, and she takes our details and says she will call back if they need to know anything else.

"Do you think they'll do anything?" I ask Sam, looking from him to my phone, just in case Natalie has sent me a message.

"No idea. It's the traditional time for drink drivers, isn't it, so they've probably got their hands full. We can but hope, though."

"Should I call Natalie, do you think?"

"I really don't know." Sam pulls the towel a little way from his nose and it looks like the flow of blood has been stemmed.

"I'm just going outside," I say. "See if there are any lights on in Natalie's house."

"There weren't," Sam says. "Stay inside, Alice. Honestly. Just in case he comes back. It's a horrible mess, but it's not our horrible mess."

"No, but she's miles away from her family…"

"I know, I know. Look, why don't you send her a message and ask her to ring you if she needs us? She might not even be there, despite what Rob said."

"I guess, though I don't know if she'll have anywhere else to go to round here. Those poor kids…"

I think of our own children and go upstairs to check on them but thankfully they are both fast asleep.

Going back downstairs, I head into the kitchen and put the kettle on, then I send Natalie a message.

I hope you're OK. I just wanted to let you know that if you need anything, Sam and I are here, and you can just call me, any time xx

If she is not at home she's going to find that a bit weird but who cares? I make two cups of decaf tea and take them into the lounge, putting the Christmas tree lights on and then snuggling down next to Sam, whose nose has stopped bleeding. I touch his cheek.

"You're cold," I say, and I pull a throw over us.

"I'm alright."

"I notice nobody else came out to help," I observe.

"No, well, people don't like to get involved, do they?"

"No. And I do get that, to a point. But when there's an angry man out there kicking reindeer, it's time to step up."

That at least gets a laugh from Sam. "Don't," he says, "I don't want my nose to start bleeding again."

"People can be scary," I say.

"Yep."

"It makes me think of Geoff."

Sam puts an arm around my shoulder. "I know. There

are some unhinged people out there. I'm sorry to say a lot of them are men. But we're not all like that."

"I know." I turn and smile at him. "Poor Natalie."

"Yep," Sam says again.

When we've drunk our tea, we head up to bed. Sam decides to try and sleep sitting up so he hopefully doesn't provoke another nose-bleed. I lie down next to him, but I know neither of us can sleep.

I hear the owl call outside and I get up and peer out of the window again. The street, I am pleased to see, is empty, and the Christmas lights are still on in my neighbours' gardens but it feels like they've lost a little of their sparkle.

8

"Have you been crying, Daddy?" Holly asks, not so much concerned as intrigued.

"No, why?"

"You got 'scara on your face like when Mummy's been crying."

Sam and I look at each other. Sam does look a bit like he's got make-up under his eye but in fact it's the bruise which is just coming out, delicate broken vessels emitting tiny blooms of blood below the surface of his skin. I'm almost more concerned, however, by her observation about me.

"Mummy doesn't cry a lot, does she?" I ask, in that annoying third-person way.

"You cried in hospital."

"Well yes, that's true." I had, almost non-stop, when I thought she couldn't see. Clearly my daughter is more observant than I gave her credit for.

"And when Julie and Luke and Zinnia went away."

"Yes, but that's because I love them and I knew how much I'd miss them."

"And sometimes in your room."

Sam looks at me again.

"Hormones," I whisper, though in honesty I just allow myself a cry from time to time, like releasing some of the pressure that builds up in me. It might sound melodramatic but it gives life to my sadness and it makes me feel less flat. I can see Sam is not convinced. Luckily, Ben chooses this moment to come in.

"Woah! Is that a black eye, Dad?" He is impressed more than concerned.

"It's… well, it's… yes," Sam flounders, grasping for a good answer but finding none. "It will be, it's just coming out."

"What happened?"

"Oh nothing exciting, I'm afraid. I wasn't fighting off bad guys or anything." Sam gives a little laugh but Ben doesn't react, just waits expectantly for the explanation. "I, well I was a bit tired in the middle of the night but I needed to go to the bathroom and I banged into the door."

"You were drunk!" Ben exclaims triumphantly.

"No, I wasn't. I was tired."

"Dad was drunk!" Ben sing-songs.

"Daddy was drunk!" Holly echoes.

And then they're chanting it together, until I tell them to stop. Sam does not look hugely amused.

"No, he wasn't drunk. I'd left the door open and Daddy didn't see it in the dark and walked right into it. You know what it's like when you wake up and you're still sleepy."

"Mm-hmm," Holly says, easily convinced.

"I still think he was drunk," Ben whispers.

"We can all hear you, Ben. But no, I wasn't," says Sam. "How could I have been? We were all watching TV together and then we all went up to bed at the same time, didn't we…?"

Ben has already lost interest and is pouring himself some cereal. I look at Sam and smile and thankfully it seems his sense of humour has returned and he smiles back.

Soon enough, Sam is off to work and I'm on my way to school with Ben and Holly. Thankfully it's a dry day and the walk clears my head. I'm feeling very tired after a sleepless night but I have a lot of work to get through today. I keep an eye out for Natalie but there's no sign of her. I'm just hoping that she and Bobby and Courtney were not home last night and will have missed Rob's behaviour. There must be something seriously amiss though, for her to have locked Rob out of their home.

When I get back to our street I pass our house and go to her front door, trying the bell but to no avail. All I can do is keep an eye out for her. Maybe I'll see her on the school run this afternoon.

Our house is quiet when I get in and I revel in the peace for a moment, going through to the kitchen where Meg looks up, slowly wagging her tail. I crouch and fuss her, and then open the back door so she can go out if she wants to. Making a cup of coffee, I take myself off to the office/playroom and get my head down. If I catch any movement outside I look up, Natalie and Rob on my mind, but there is no sign of either of them.

Come the school run, still no sign – and when I ask Ben and Holly if they've seen Bobby or Courtney they say no, but then they're not in the same classes so they might not have seen them anyway.

"I'm so tired, Mummy," Holly says and I of course check my phone to make sure her sugar levels are OK. They're fine. It's just the time of year.

"Me too, sweetie. I can't wait for Wednesday and school holidays!"

"Yay! And Christmas."

"And Christmas," I agree.

"Don't forget Granny and Grandpa are coming later though."

"Oh," says Ben.

"What's up, Ben?" I ask. "Don't you want them to?"

"It's not that. I was just – I just want to be quiet tonight."

"I understand. Don't worry, they won't be staying long. They're just coming to say bye and wish us a happy Christmas, before they go on holiday."

"I already wished them a happy Christmas," he says.

"Well yes, that's OK. Don't worry, you don't have to talk to them if you don't want to," I snap, feeling protective towards my parents and also knowing – which Ben doesn't – that they are coming to drop off his and Holly's presents which, if previous years are anything to go by, there will be far too many of.

As it is, once he's had a sit down and something to eat, Ben is really happy to see Mum and Dad and they spend some time building a marble run, together with Holly. While they are occupied, I ferry the numerous bags of presents in from the car and upstairs.

I have to get quite inventive with my hiding spaces, given that Sam and I have already wrapped and hidden the presents from us, and from Father Christmas. Did I used to get this many presents? I don't think so, though I certainly never went without.

Mum has given me strict instructions as to the wrapping, which will help identify which are Holly's and which are

Ben's. "There were so many I didn't have enough name tags!"

"I'm not surprised."

"But luckily I had the different types of wrapping paper already so it should be obvious whose is whose. Oh and yours and Sam's are labelled."

"Mum!" I'd laughed. "How many are there?"

"Oh, just a few. Just bits and pieces I've picked up through the year. And Holly's birthday presents are all in birthday paper so that makes that easy."

"Just bits and pieces," I mutter to myself as I make my third trip up the stairs.

"What was that, darling?" my sharp-eared mum calls.

"Nothing!"

I manage to ram – I mean carefully conceal – the last bag behind some of the clothes in my wardrobe. I hope I can remember where everything is.

And then it's time for tea, and then time for Mum and Dad to say goodbye. We go out onto the driveway and I can't help glancing along the street towards Natalie's house. I see there's a light on behind drawn curtains so I guess that she's back. At least I hope it's her and not Rob.

"We'd better get cracking." Dad jangles his keys, never one for protracted goodbyes.

"Have a lovely time," I say.

"Oh you too, Alice," Mum hugs me tightly. "We'll miss you. I wish we weren't going…"

"No you don't!" I laugh. "You'll have a brilliant time."

"Yes we will miss you, and we will have a brilliant time," says Dad. "Come on Sue, we're keeping these children out of their beds. Good luck with the plays tomorrow, or break a leg, I should say."

Holly looks horrified.

"It's just a saying, Holly," Mum explains. "Make sure your mummy sends me a video, OK? And tell your daddy I hope he has a very happy Christmas as well."

"OK Granny." Holly lets out a huge yawn, which makes us laugh.

"That's our cue then," says Mum, and she gets into the car, then Dad does the same and we wave them off as they head away down the street and towards their adventure.

"Come on then you two, time for bed," I say, and just for once neither of my children protest.

9

This morning the children can talk of little but their Christmas plays. Holly, a narrator, had initially been very disappointed when she was told what part she would play. Her role means wearing smart clothes but it's not exactly glamorous. However, realising it means she is present for every scene, she has warmed to the concept. Where she gets her extrovert nature from, I have no idea. It's certainly not me or Sam. Although – "Oh I don't know, Alice," Mum had said when I'd voiced this thought to her. "You used to be quite the little actress in your day. Didn't she, Phil?"

"Oh yes love, don't you remember how you used to make our visitors watch you perform? You used to pretend our patio doors were the front of stage and you'd pull the curtains across then appear from behind them, demanding applause."

Mum had giggled at this and I'd felt my face flushing at these long-forgotten memories. I think maybe I was a bit of an attention-seeker; an only child constantly on the hunt for adult approval. In fact, as I remember it now, Nigel Simpkins was one such adult and was always very kind. I seem to remember him bringing me some play scripts once, and patiently practising them with me. Poor guy – he probably just wanted to put his feet up after work and to enjoy a bit of grown-up company!

So perhaps this side of Holly does actually come from me. Ben would retreat from the thought of such individual attention, however; it is strictly safety in numbers for him. He is definitely letting the power go to his head though, with this new lofty position of Centurion. He marches up and down now, practising his lines and swinging his imaginary sword around.

"You'll need to watch out when you've got your actual sword in your hand," I say. I am not sure it was the wisest choice for the school to let their Roman soldiers have plastic weapons but there you go.

"I'll be careful," Ben says crossly, and I imagine he'd make a good centurion. He'd take no messing from his troops, that's for sure.

On the way to school I keep an eye out for Natalie, as I had done yesterday. Without wishing to be a nosy neighbour but wanting to be a concerned friend – though I'm not sure I've been that good a friend to her – I have kept an occasional eye on their house and their driveway. I have not seen Natalie or the kids, or Rob for that matter, and the driveway has remained free of his car.

Today, we walk all the way to school just the three of us and it strikes me as ironic that I normally want it to be this way but today I would very much like to see Natalie. Just to make sure she's OK.

As it happens, I do catch a glimpse of her but it's not till we get to school and she is disappearing off across the playground, holding Courtney's hand. I am about to go after her with Holly, Ben having already run off with his mates, when I hear a voice behind me.

"Alice! Alice, how are you?" If my heart had sunk a little the other day when Natalie had caught up with me, now it drops right to my feet. I know this voice. It belongs to none other than Belinda Carmichael – "Nearly Belinda Carlisle," she always quips when she introduces herself. She has a boy, Tristram, in Holly's class, and a girl, Jemima, in Ben's, so there really is no escaping her.

"Hi Belinda," I say, holding on to Holly's hand and fighting the urge to make a run for it.

"How *are* you?" she asks again, with this 'concerned' expression on her face as she looks down towards Holly. "And how are you my darling? How's the *diabetes*?" She looks back to me and whispers the last word.

I mean – how do I answer that? *It's amazing thanks, Belinda. Brilliant. We're all loving it.*

"Oh we're managing fine aren't we, Holly?"

Holly looks up at me. She isn't upset by talking about diabetes; if anything I think she finds it a bit boring. She's got better things to think about.

"Oh you are such a brave girl," Belinda says, crouching down.

"Well yes she is but you're OK aren't you, Holly?" I ask. "It's just something extra to think about."

Holly remains quiet.

"Yeah it's alright thanks Belinda," I say, seeing her wide eyes on me and kicking myself for filling the silence when I don't need to. "Holly's got an insulin pump and a continuous glucose sensor and…"

"Oh I'm so sorry to stop you there," Belinda interjects and I notice her eyes have glazed over slightly, "but I've really got to talk to Trish. But if there's anything I can do, Alice…"

Her eyes meet mine with a look of such faux sympathy, I want to say, "Sure. You can stop leaving Holly out of party invites because you think diabetes is 'too difficult to cater for'." Yes, I've heard her actually say that, although she didn't realise I did. It hurt like a blow to the stomach. But that weekend we went out with Mum and Dad, to the Zuper Zoo, which Holly loves, and she was blissfully unaware she'd been left out of anything. Until, that is, she went back to school and her friends were talking about what a wonderful time they'd had.

If there's anything I can do… Are they the most empty words on the planet? Or do people actually mean them? It depends on who's saying them I suppose, but in Belinda's case I can't help thinking they're a meaningless utterance which lets her feel she's done something good without having to do anything at all.

There is a good chance, of course, that I'm a bit touchy about all this and need to settle down and get things back in perspective. Whatever anyone else does, what's important is our family and the long-term. People at school will come and go. I think perhaps these things get to me more than they might because I spend so much more time on my own these days. Little gripes and niggles which I'd have had to brush off before and laugh about with Julie seem to worm their way in, burrowing deep into the recesses of my mind and worrying at me as I sit at my desk, with nobody to talk to but Meg. *Look on the bright side*, I tell myself, *you don't want to talk to Belinda anyway.*

"Sure, no problem," I say, and make a mental note that getting into the technical details is a good way to move

73

Belinda on. I mean, maybe she does care in her way but I am also aware that she likes to be in on everything, and takes a little bit of delight in other people's misfortune. It gives her something to gossip about. I know she was one of the people responsible for spreading the word about Holly being diabetic, so that for a while everywhere I went people would ask me about it. It wasn't what I needed, to be honest, and definitely not what I wanted for Holly. I need it not to be the first thing people ask about or talk to her about. It needs to just sink into place as part of everyday life, for her and for us. I also don't want people offering sympathy – fake or otherwise – to her about it. She cannot go through life feeling sorry for herself.

I squeeze Holly's hand and smile at her. "Let's get you into class before the bell goes, shall we?"

We scoot across the playground and she goes straight into the lobby in front of her classroom. I hand over her diabetes kit, including mobile phone, to Miss Atkins, the teaching assistant who manages Holly's diabetes stuff while she's in school.

"I didn't even wish her luck for the play!" I say. "Can you pass it on please?"

"Of course," Miss Atkins smiles.

"Just don't say break a leg please, my dad said that to her and she looked terrified!"

I leave the playground with a spring in my step. I love the school that Ben and Holly go to, and the people who work there. And I also love the view from up here. It's incredible. Today, which just happens to be the winter solstice, it's clear and fresh, and the sea is a glistening expanse. Whatever the weather, I always feel its pull and most days I have to press on, back home to the office, but today I am answering its call. In the absence of Lizzie and her celebrations, I am treating myself to a solstice sea swim.

***

It is quiet at the beach, just a handful of dog walkers and a white-haired couple holding hands as they traverse the seashore. As I walk my gaze is firmly on the water, just in case of dolphins. It's not unknown for them to be in the bay at any time of year and it feels like they should be here today to add an extra touch of magic.

No such luck though, but there are plenty of seabirds to admire, and a shiny seal's head bobbing up and down. Is it watching me?

I have chosen the most sheltered beach, which is where I take Ben and Holly if they want to have a splash about. Today the tide is halfway in so I walk to the point where the sand shelves more sharply away and I pull off my joggers and hoodie. I blow up my tow float and fasten it around my waist and then I go for it. There's no other way. I tuck the float under my arm and I jog down and into the sea, which is surprisingly – well OK, 'warm' is a bit of an exaggeration, let's just go with 'not as cold as you might expect'.

"Keep going, Alice," I say to myself, looking left and right to see if there are any other swimmers but no, it's just me right now.

There is a large cloud currently passing the sun but as I splash water over my neck and shoulders, trying to acclimatise, the sun breaks free and the world is a bright burst of colour again. I see the hotels and houses up behind the station, dark windows like eyes peering down at me.

Above them, the sky is a deep, vivid blue. Down here, the sea is so clear and the sand on the beach looks almost white as the sun's rays bounce off it. The slight tang of salt is on my lips and my tongue. I take the plunge, and I'm swimming.

I breathe deep and slow at first to make sure my body and mind remain calm but as soon as I feel OK, I push myself forward, front-crawling half the length of the beach parallel to the shore. I haven't gone out too deep, for fear of unseen currents stealing me away, but I don't need to go a long way out, just as long as it's deep enough to swim.

It's different in the summer, with the reassuring presence of the lifeguards, but I am more aware of my vulnerability these days – and of my necessity in other people's lives. That's not me having an inflated ego; it's just that I am a mum – already a position of huge responsibility and not to be taken lightly – and on top of that I hold an awful lot of knowledge in my head about managing Holly's health. I am my parents' only child and their main support. So as well as self-preservation purely because I value my health and my life, I do know that my sudden absence from people's lives would affect theirs enormously.

They would come back from it, I'm sure. I know that Sam would step up, and I realise I haven't even thought of him in my list of people who depend on me. That, I think, is because I can also depend on him. We are partners in the truest sense of the word. So if I did happen to drop off my perch I know there's a safety net in place. Even so, I'd rather not, thanks very much.

I pause this train of thought and hear Lizzie's voice in my mind. *Be in the moment. Breathe.* I stop and I turn towards the horizon, treading water. I see the seal about ten metres away, then it vanishes under the surface and I try to guess where it will pop up next. As long as it's not right next to me. I love the seals, and I love being able to share the sea with them, but when all's said and done this is their home and perhaps they're not always in the mood for sharing.

I guess wrong and I see the dark, shiny head pop up again about ten metres to my left, closer to the town. It will probably head off towards the harbour at some point, when the fishing boats are coming in.

I let my feet rise to the surface, my body facing upwards, and I hold onto my float, feeling a little bit like an otter as I let the waves lift and lower me. Then slowly I lower my head back, gasping at the shock of the cold on my scalp then relaxing as my hair fans out around my head and shoulders and my ears fill with salty bubbles while I gaze at the sky.

I shouldn't be too long, I know; I don't want to get cold, and I also need to get home to work. I must be finished today in time to get to school for the plays. Imagine my children's indignance if I missed them! It doesn't bear thinking about.

I take my time swimming back until I am parallel with the place I left my bag, and then reluctantly I allow my feet to come into contact with the sand and I begin the slow walk out and back to reality. The sea holds me back at first, like it doesn't want me to leave, but as more and more of my body emerges, tiny saltwater rivulets running over my skin, it has less of a grip on me. I'm grateful for this chance to have come here and I send out solstice wishes to Lizzie and Julie, both so far away, hoping that they know I am thinking of them and missing our Amethi solstice celebrations. Missing them.

As I reach the shallows, I watch the little rainbows which appear as my feet kick up droplets of water, and I turn once more to the horizon, scanning the waves, just in case, but it's not to be. No dolphins today. Nevertheless, the seal chooses that moment to bob up again, this time closer to the rocks and, ridiculous though it sounds, it feels like we make eye contact. *Thank you*, I think, hoping it can somehow sense and understand my thoughts. *Thank you for sharing the sea with me.*

Yep, I'm definitely losing it.

10

My careful plotting of the day works, I'm happy to say. I allow myself a block of two hours to work after my return home and warming shower; half an hour for lunch and a short walk with Meg; a further hour to work, and then I am on my way to school. Sam has messaged to say he's got stuck with something at the office and he's not going to be able to make it in time for the plays but Karen and Ron are going to meet me at the school.

There is already quite a queue of parents, grandparents and carers forming in the playground and as I walk along I see Natalie is near the front of the line but she is deep in conversation with another woman so she doesn't notice me. I greet a few of the other parents and see Ron and Karen are about halfway along.

"Alice!" Karen calls excitedly and pointedly says, "We saved you a place."

"Oh, erm," I look apologetically at the man and woman directly behind them. They just smile and indicate I should accept Karen's offer.

Ron puts his hand on my shoulder. "Good day so far?"

"Not bad, thank you Ron. I had a swim this morning."

"I thought you were working?" Karen, sharp as a tack, says. "You always say that you're working all the hours the kids are in school."

I grit my teeth, "Yes, I do normally, but I allowed myself an hour off this morning for a solstice swim."

"Solstice!" Karen says and rolls her eyes.

"That sounds nice, Alice," Ron says diplomatically. "I bet it was a lovely morning for it. And I'm sure you need a bit of time to yourself every now and then."

"It did do me good," I say. "Cleared my head."

"Well good for you," Karen says, "and don't worry, we won't tell Shona."

"She knows I went for a swim!" I exclaim. "I wasn't bunking off. I just invoice her for the hours I work."

"It sounds like a good set-up," Ron says approvingly.

"It is," I admit. "I'm lucky."

"But you're missing Amethi?" Karen asks, suddenly and surprisingly more understanding. "And Julie?"

"Yes. Very much."

"It's a shame."

"I know. But it can't be helped."

At that moment, the queue begins to move forward and I fish our tickets out of my inside pocket.

Karen tuts as she looks at hers. "I don't know why they had to introduce numbering."

"I suppose it's just to keep things organised," I say. "And to stop any disputes over who sits where." I leave it at that.

As we walk into the hall, holding mugs of tea and biscuits made by the year sixes, I see that my allocated seat is next to Natalie. I also see that the seat to her left is empty. Presumably for Rob. Will he be making an appearance?

"Hi Natalie," I say as I shuffle along next to her.

"Oh, hi." She looks at me then busies herself reading the programme. I am quite sure it doesn't require as much attention as she's giving it and I don't know if she is giving me the cold shoulder or if she's embarrassed about the other night. Neither is necessary, though I do feel bad about letting her down at the weekend.

Karen and Ron are fiddling about with a large camera and then Karen spots somebody she knows and makes Ron and the people next to him stand up so she can go across to talk to them but then the headteacher, Mrs Lambert, comes in and the room goes quiet except for Karen who is saying, "Excuse me," and "Sorry!" as she makes everyone stand up again so she can return to her seat, just as the children begin to file in.

It's the youngest children first, which means that Holly and Natalie's daughter Courtney are up. Holly is sharing her narrator role with her friend Joby and the pair of them sit neatly, very composed, on two chairs at the side of the stage. They take it in turns to tell the story, which is all in rhyme, about a pair of mice in a house on Christmas Eve, while their classmates come on stage in costume. It is all very sweet, with lots of singing and dancing. I glance at Natalie when Courtney's up, dancing like a twinkling star, and I notice Natalie's eyes are shining. She looks my way and we actually share a smile. I want to put a hand on her arm, to congratulate her on her lovely daughter, and to somehow convey that everything will be OK, but I don't feel like I can.

I know my own eyes are shining too at times as I watch my daughter confidently deliver her lines and I consider how lucky we are to have her. I try not to think this too much but in times gone by diabetes would have been a death sentence. As it is, I sometimes struggle with the fear that we are just a step or two away from catastrophe, every single day. It's not a healthy line of thought, and it's completely redundant. We just have to keep going. Keep the medical supplies stocked up. Change the insulin in the pump and Holly's cannula every three days. Change the sensor every ten days. Keep track of what Holly is eating. Make adjustments for illness or exercise or even hot weather. These are some of the many things we have to consider to keep our little girl healthy and well. But we do, and we can, and diabetes is no longer a death sentence, or anything like it. There is no reason that a person with diabetes should not live a long and happy life; it just takes a bit more work and thought in order to do so. Still, it gets me, seeing her up there, and I swallow back my tears and stare down at my hands until it's safe to look up again without fear of openly sobbing.

When it's the older children's play and Ben and Bobby are both on stage, I look Natalie's way again but this time she doesn't look back. Instead, I turn to Karen and she grins at me. "He's very good," she says, a bit too loudly, but I reason that if there is any place to be a proud grandparent it's in a room full of other proud grandparents and parents.

Ben does seem to relish his role as a centurion. He is taller than all of his troops and he's clearly been primed to be straight-backed. He speaks his lines with an air of authority and I find myself grinning from ear to ear.

What a thing it is to be a parent. These are the moments to hold onto, and remember. The shiny fruits of all the hard work and the stress and the worry, the self-doubt and the sleepless nights. But that's not to say the day-to-day parenting doesn't have its own rewards. The unexpected smiles or spontaneous kitchen discos. The heartfelt hugs, and belly laughs. One day these children of mine are going to be all grown up and I can't imagine a life without them at home and in my world every single day. So it's not really just these moments we should hold onto – the Christmas plays, the sports days, the assemblies and music recitals – but every moment we can. And I know I'm getting over-emotional because it's Christmas and there are sweet little children singing in their innocent voices, and one of the reception boys has actually fallen asleep down there on the floor, and a girl in year one is crying about something in her dad's arms. But really, these are the days, aren't they? Children are the people that matter. Unformed and untainted by all the unhealthy things that adults feel the need to drag into their lives. The world we create is the world they grow into and I can't help but feel sometimes like we are letting them down.

I sob suddenly, from the power of all these thoughts rushing through me, and I see Natalie's head turn sharply but now I can't look at her. I am too intent on not dissolving into tears and ending up on the floor, a pathetic, snivelling wreck.

After all the applause has died down and the children have returned to their classrooms to get their bags and school uniforms, the adults begin to file out of the hall.

"God, that got me really badly this year," I say to Natalie.

"I noticed," she smiles and I feel like something has thawed between us.

"I'm really sorry about the weekend," I say.

"It's not your fault." She stiffens slightly.

"I just – I wondered if maybe you and your two would like to do something tomorrow afternoon, celebrate the end of term? You can just come round for tea if you like."

"We can't," she says shortly, adding almost as an afterthought, "sorry."

And then she sees Courtney and she's dashing across the room to pick her little girl up and congratulate her, and then Karen's calling me across to see Holly, who has just emerged from her classroom, and Ben and his friends are whizzing about like Tasmanian devils, and I have to try and contain him and calm him down, and by the time I have a chance to look for her again, Natalie has gone.

Ah well, it probably serves me right for turning down her invites in the past. And for letting her down at the weekend. And besides, it's not like I have wanted to spend time with her. But now that the boot's on the other foot and it's Natalie turning me down, I don't like it. Pathetic, but true.

Ron drives us all back home in his Land Rover Discovery, which Ben and Holly love. We pile into the house, greeted by Meg, who looks a little more lively and spritely than she has recently. It's lovely to see as she snuffles around us all, tail wagging.

"Maybe it's you, Ron," I say as Meg really presses her head against his leg.

"Well it's always nice to see her," says Ron and he sits on the bottom step to fuss her. "Two old-timers together, eh?"

I see Karen gazing at Ron with such love I feel a flood of warmth for her. She's a funny one, my mother-in-law; a bit sharp around the edges but I know she's got a soft centre, and I really know how much she loves Ben and Holly.

"Tea?" I ask her, and she follows me through to the kitchen.

"How is everything, Alice?" she asks.

"It's fine," I say, picking up the kettle from the stand and flashing her a smile.

"Honestly? I noticed you were close to tears at school."

"Oh you know, school plays and..." But she has ambushed me with her directness and with her unexpected observation. "I'm just tired, I guess."

"Still getting up in the night with Holly?"

"No, not really, or not so much now we've got the sensor, and the app, and well, nights are much better..."

"But you can't stop checking everything's OK?"

"No," I admit. "I can't." And it's true. While I am getting more sleep, thanks to this incredibly clever technology, there is a small part of me that finds it hard to entrust my little girl's health and wellbeing to it. And if I wake in the night – which I do, most nights – I have to check my phone, look at her glucose reading. And sometimes, on particularly restless nights, I will sneak through and perform a finger-prick test on her, which she is so used to she doesn't even stir, just to make sure things really are OK. Am I damaged? Neurotic? Traumatised?

I voice these questions to Karen.

"No, my lovely, you are just a mum, and a damned good one." She steps forward and holds me in a vicelike hug. "I'm so grateful Sam found you. And that Ben and Holly have got you."

Oh my god, I'm in tears again. And so is Karen.

Ron walks through and looks worried. "Everything OK, ladies?"

"Yes," we both say, stepping back and looking at each other.

"Just Christmas, you know. It's all a bit emotional," I explain.

"I know Karen's felt bad about going away at this time of year," Ron says, stepping forward and putting an arm around her.

"You mustn't," I say. "I know how much Janie and Jonathan are looking forward to having you with them this year. And you're always here for us. We know that."

Karen wipes her eyes. "Thank you, Alice."

We take our cups of tea through to the lounge, where Ben makes us sit through all his lines again and cajoles Holly into being one of his soldiers. I sense he is reluctant to relinquish the power he's been enjoying. When he goes into school tomorrow he'll just be Ben again.

The four of them settle down to watch one of the CBeebies pantomimes and I put some pasta on and stick some garlic bread in the oven. "Homemade sauce though, Julie," I mutter, chopping onions and garlic into such minuscule bits that they won't be noticed by the children's incredibly sensitive palates and gag reflexes. I open a couple of cans of tomatoes, add some vegetable stock and basil, and let it all bubble away while I grate some cheese. Just as the pasta is about ready to drain, Sam gets home and is greeted enthusiastically by us all.

We sit down to a cosy family meal, at Holly's insistence by just the lights of the Christmas tree. And, though the pasta is hardly festive, we have Christmas crackers and put on the colourful paper hats, laughing at the terrible jokes. It's a lovely evening but the children are tired and so are Sam and I. By half-seven it's time to call it a night, and I go out to the Land Rover with Ron to sneakily get the presents they have brought with them.

"Bloody hell!" I exclaim at the sight of the bags and boxes in the light of his boot.

"I know. Karen can't help herself," he says fondly. "Mind you, I've picked out a few of these things myself, you know."

"Well that's so lovely of you both, Ron," I say, and I hug him.

"Steady on," he laughs, but I can tell he's pleased.

We cart the presents in and upstairs, checking that the door to the lounge is closed so that the children don't see us.

"Where do you want them?" Ron asks.

I look around slightly helplessly. "Erm... in our room?" I will have to pull out the suitcases that we keep under the bed and hope that I can fit Ron and Karen's gifts in there.

"Right you are. Now, Karen gave me some instructions about whose presents are wrapped in which paper. She said she'd been talking to Sue, who told her that's what she and Phil did, and it saved on labels so..."

Oh god, now I've got another lot of unlabelled presents to remember which is destined for which child, and who has given them. I need to make a note of all this.

"Thank you Ron," I say as he shows me, and then we go back downstairs. He and Karen get their coats and shoes and Sam and I carry a child each outside to wave them off.

"Merry Christmas!" we shout as they head off down the road, Ron sticking his arm out of the window and waving.

I look at Sam as we turn to head back inside. "That's both lots of grandparents gone then," I say.

"It's going to be strange without them."

"But," I counter, thinking we need to keep things upbeat, "we are going to have such a cosy Christmas, just the four of us and Meg, aren't we kids?"

"Yeah!" Holly says.

"Yes," Ben replies, wriggling to get down and out of Sam's arms now that his grandparents have gone and he's remembered he is actually a very grown-up boy these days.

"And my birthday!" pipes up Holly.

"And your birthday, of course," agrees Sam, and she reaches her arms out towards him. He carries her straight upstairs and Ben follows on while I shut the front door, feeling the warmth of our home fold itself around me.

11

Finally. It's the last day of the school term. I pack the kids off to school in their non-uniform, Ben having begged me to gel his hair for him and then Holly having begged me for two French plaits "like 'melia has" only for her to hate them and demand that I undo all my painstaking work and leave her hair down, just as it had been half an hour earlier.

By the time we're ready it's getting late and I end up caving in and driving. I don't like to do this because the school is so close, and it's the wrong choice environmentally, but it also means I will miss my walk and chance to wallow in my own thoughts. I rely on that sacred time, and this is the main reason I become irritated when Natalie or anyone else intrudes on it. It's nothing personal really, although I can see how I haven't been the friendliest or most welcoming of companions.

After I've deposited the children safely, I see Natalie walking on her own along the street on her way home so I slow down and open my window. "Want a lift?"

She pretty much jumps out of her skin at the sound of my voice. She turns, and her face reddens.

"Oh. No thanks."

"I don't blame you. I hate driving this short journey," I say. "Maybe see you later?"

"Yes, maybe."

Is it my imagination or is she still being off with me? I don't know. Maybe it's best just to leave her to it.

When I get in, I open the door for Meg to go outside and we have a half-hearted game of fetch. I feel like she's doing it more to please me than for her own enjoyment so I sit on the back doorstep and she comes for a cuddle instead. That seems to be more her speed these days.

I hear my phone going and pull it out of my pocket. It's Julie, on a video call.

"Hello!" I grin as her face appears on my phone screen. I keep stroking Meg with one hand and hold my phone away so Julie can see us both.

"Alice!" she cries. "And Meg! Oh but she looks old."

"I know, I guess she is. But she's still a beauty, aren't you?" Meg looks up and licks my chin.

"Always," says Julie. "So how are you? Kids broken up yet?"

"Not yet, it's the last day today. How about Zinnie?"

"Yep, she's off now. She's still in bed at the moment."

"Of course. It must be stupidly early there!"

"Yeah, well Mum and Lee's flight gets in really early and I'm off to the airport to get them soon. I just had a few spare minutes so I thought I'd waste them talking to you."

"Thanks, I think. I bet Zinnie's excited."

"Oh my god, just a bit. But they're going to be knackered so I'm packing her off to her friend Macy's today, just to give our guests a chance to acclimatise before they get jumped all over."

"Ahh that's nice." Inside, a part of me feels jealous on

behalf of my kids. Zinnia should be with them, not Macy, whoever she is. But does that mean I wish Zinnia hadn't made friends in Canada? Would I prefer her to be alone and lonely? Of course not.

"It's going to be pretty magical having them here. And snow's forecast for tonight."

"A white Christmas! Amazing."

"Takes me a back a few years," says Julie.

"Me too. I don't think it's going to be like that this year though. Just sort of damp and unsatisfying. Hang on," I say. "Weather Talk."

Julie and I have always been a bit disparaging of conversations which revolve around the weather, although I do recognise that it's sometimes the only thing people have in common. But on a hot day – or cold day – or if it's windy, or rainy – we worked out that you will end up having to talk about it with at least five people in the school playground, or passers-by on the street, or customers on the phone. Julie and I try to avoid it if we can.

"So tell me something interesting instead," Julie says.

"OK, I will. But just hang on, I'll go inside."

"Yes, you don't want the neighbours hearing. News travels fast in a small town like Summer Bay," Julie says.

"It sure does." I stand up and straighten my knees and back, trying not to emit a groan as I often do these days. "Come on Meg," I coax her inside and shut the door.

"Well, it's actually about one of my neighbours," I say very quietly.

"You don't have to whisper now, Alice," Julie laughs.

"Oh yeah, sorry. I just always feel like people might be listening."

"Google? Amazon? Unplug your Alexa."

"We haven't got one."

"You should be ok then. So go on…"

I relay what happened with Rob the other night and Julie gasps when I tell her Sam has a black eye – "Bet he looks even sexier now," she laughs.

"Hey, keep your hands off my man."

"Sorry. Carry on."

"Yeah, well now there's been no sign of Rob and when I've seen Natalie she's pretty much giving me the cold shoulder."

"But isn't that a good thing? I thought you found her annoying?"

"Well yes, and no. I mean, that's just me being a miserable bugger. And she's just not you, is she?"

"Correct," Julie says. "You shall have no friends who are not me. Stay faithful, Alice. Wait for me."

"I would if I thought you'd come back," I say wistfully and immediately regret it. I don't actually want to make Julie feel bad. "But I don't know. It's not like Natalie's not a nice person. And I think that now I can see what her relationship might be like, I have more of an idea of why she is how she is."

"Well, yeah. If anyone knows what she might be going through, it's you. I remember that Christmas, when you and I were meant to be going out partying and Geoff wouldn't let you."

Thinking of that time makes my stomach feel like it's twisting up. I imagine it as a handkerchief being wrung out tightly. "Don't remind me."

"He was a wrong'un, Alice, and it sounds like Rob might be too."

"Yeah but now Natalie doesn't want to talk to me."

"You don't know that. Not really. As you said, she might just be embarrassed. Maybe you should give her a couple of days. See if she wants to get together over Christmas."

"Well I guess she might go up to her mum's now Rob seems to be out of the picture, though I don't know how she'll get there. She can't drive and you know what trains are like at Christmas."

"Yeah – terrible on your own and an absolute nightmare with kids. Poor woman," Julie says.

"Yeah. I'll just see how things go. I'll keep an eye out for her."

"And her husband."

"Yep. Maybe we've seen the last of him."

"Let's hope so."

I feel buoyed up after my chat with Julie and we promise to talk at some time on Christmas Day. I make a cup of coffee and a piece of toast then head to my desk and I work my way through all my emails – responding, deleting and filing them away as appropriate. By the time I am done, it's two o'clock and I haven't had any lunch. I call Shona to check in before I clock off, then maybe I can have an hour all to myself before I get the kids and the Christmas mayhem begins.

"Thank you Alice," Shona smiles.

"What for?"

"Just for taking care of everything so well. Honestly, you don't know what a relief it is to me. I love this business. It's my baby, for want of a better word. I know that's such a cliché. But I started this up when I was on my own and I couldn't trust just anyone to work with me, you know."

I feel immensely flattered. "Well thank you. I really appreciate that."

"I was thinking maybe next year, if you feel ready for it, you can get out and about a bit more. Meet a few clients. Get some of your own. If it fits in with life, I mean. Only if you're comfortable with it, Alice."

"Oh, I… I'd love that."

"Really? That would be fantastic for me. I think Si's going to have a busy year you know, and Lydia's not going to have as much time to support him."

"Oh?"

"Yes, but maybe I've said too much. I… Oh bugger it. Don't tell them I told you, OK?"

"OK…"

"They're having a baby," she hisses with evident relief at being able to release this news to somebody.

"No way!" I think of Lydia, the seventeen-year-old who came to work for me at the Sail Loft and went on to ace her A-levels, then her degree, and then came back to Cornwall to manage the Bay Hotel. She held her own with Si; not easy when you've got a drop-dead gorgeous A-list actor pursuing you, and over the last year she's taken on Amethi, building on what Julie and I created to make it a self-contained retreat. I've heard amazing things about what she's doing; all her events are a sell-out, although I suppose that Si's occasional presence may be a bit of a draw – not that they advertise it, but it's hard to keep that kind of thing quiet. And now she's going to be a mum.

I remember my own first pregnancy when I was at Amethi and all those beautiful, idyllic imaginings I'd had of having my baby snoozing rosy-cheeked in a basket by my desk or in a sling as I did the rounds. It didn't work out quite like that of course but it will be different for Lydia, I hope. She has a reliable set of staff who can keep things going. I want to message her now and tell her how pleased I am but of course I can't. I'm not supposed to know.

"It's maybe not very professional of me, Alice, but I've been bursting to tell somebody. And I'm informing you as a trusted colleague, not a friend, OK?"

"OK," I smile. These lines are quite blurry sometimes. "It's actually lovely to hear some good news anyway."

"Oh? Everything OK?"

"Yeah, it's fine. Just a... friend... having a tough time. Dragging up some painful memories for me as well."

"I'm sorry to hear that, Alice. If you ever want to talk – as colleagues or as friends – then you know where I am."

"Thank you." I appreciate that, although as she's just told me Si and Lydia's secret I will think twice before telling her any of mine.

"Now switch off and get ready for the holidays!" Shona says. "Work can wait. We're looking forward to seeing you on Christmas Eve."

"We're looking forward to it too! We probably won't stay very late as the kids will be desperate to get ready for Santa."

"Of course, of course. Oh, and Alice?"

"Yes?"

"Check your bank. There's a little Christmas gift in it."

"You shouldn't have! Thank you, Shona."

"You deserve it. It's been a good year and a lot of that is thanks to you."

As soon as the call is ended, I log onto my banking app. £1000! I had expected maybe £100 at the most. This is going to make the Christmas expenses easier to manage. What with this bonus from Shona and the ever-growing piles of presents in every nook and cranny of the house, I feel very lucky indeed.

12

And they're off! Ben and Holly are off school and out of their minds with Christmas excitement. They've found their empty Christmas stockings (actually rugby socks, and we have the matching socks already stuffed full of presents which rustle pleasingly when moved – this is unusually well organised for me and Sam but it's a good feeling) and I have had to stop them swinging them around their heads and hitting each other with them.

Holly has burst into tears three times and Ben once. It's time to get out of the house.

"Who wants to go to Zuper Zoo?" I ask.

"Yes!" Holly shouts. "Yes, yes, yes."

"Sure," Ben says, reverting to playing it cool. I'm going to have to keep an eye on him while he's growing up.

"Come on then." I feel frivolous, secure in the knowledge we have extra cash thanks to Shona, and beginning to feel a little bit of the spirit of Christmas myself. I would normally be frantically putting sandwiches together, grabbing crisps and biscuits and fruit, but today I think I'll treat them to something at the café. And tonight we're eating out, so this is shaping up to be a great day.

There is Christmas music being pumped out of the speakers around Zuper Zoo, and it's clear that I'm not the only person desperate to get the kids out of the house. It is heaving, and all around us tempers are fraying but being kept in check as harassed parents remind themselves it's Christmas and it's meant to be a happy time. Are we all just looking forward to Boxing Day?

But Ben and Holly are on good form, I'm pleased to say after their earlier antics, and they hold hands as we go around the zoo. I feel very proud and a little bit smug but I know this is a dangerous line to be walking and that we could fall off at any given moment.

Holly loves the giant tortoises, Ben loves the lynxes, and they both love the meerkats, so we spend an awful lot of time at their enclosure. It's just as I'm trying to get a photo without either of my children noticing, with a perfect background of a meerkat standing upright at the top of a log, that I hear a familiar voice. Oh no.

Rob.

What's he doing here? Well of course he's got the kids. Is Natalie here too? He hasn't seen me yet I realise as I tuck my phone into my pocket and straighten up.

"Oh, hi," he says. "Great minds, eh?"

"Erm…" Why is he acting like nothing's happened? I suppose it's a bit awkward with all four of our children present. Courtney runs up to Holly and they hug, while Ben and Bobby immediately begin a game of chase, laughing and pulling at each other's sleeves.

"Careful you two!" I call. "So how are you?" I ask, automated good manners kicking in.

"Good thanks, Alice. Good. Yourself?" It feels like I'm talking to somebody at work.

"Oh, you know…"

What the hell am I supposed to say? *You hit my husband! You called your wife a bitch. You're a nasty piece of work.*

Luckily Rob seems to sense my discomfort. "Right, yes, well. Come on kids!"

"Ohhh," Courtney says. "Can't I stay with Holly? Can we have lunch together?"

"Yes! Please. Can we Mummy?" Holly asks.

"I don't think so, sorry, we're going to have to go before lunch."

"But you said we were going to the café!"

"Yes, I didn't mean this one. I meant the Cross-Section." Our friend Chris's upmarket restaurant is the first place that sprang to mind.

"Cross-Section! Yay! Can Courtney come?"

Thankfully, Rob steps in. "She can't, sorry, we're on a tight budget."

"Yes, well it's just a bit of a treat. And we know the owner," I say.

"Alright for some." He calls Bobby and takes Courtney's hand and they're gone, leaving me feeling both uncomfortable and annoyed.

"We're going to Cross-Section!" Holly tells Ben.

"Brilliant!" Ben says.

What have I done? That Christmas bonus isn't going to last long if I carry on this way.

As it is, I'm pleased with our choice. We passed the café at Zuper Zoo on our way out. It was rammed and I experienced a small amount of satisfaction to see a stressed-looking Rob in the queue. I just hope he doesn't take it out on the kids.

On the drive towards the estuary and the restaurant, I replay the meeting with Natalie's husband. It's made me uncomfortable. Does it mean he's back home? It is none of my business, of course, but I am not very happy to think we might have to live in close proximity to the man who punched Sam and, more than that, I worry for Natalie. I just think if he's the type to shout and punch and call her horrible names once, he will do it again – and presumably he has done it before. But what can I do?

When we get to the restaurant we are greeted by Christian himself. "I just wondered if you had a table for us?" I say. "I realise it's a bit silly just turning up at lunchtime this close to Christmas."

"Alice, I would always try to find a table for you if I could but we're so busy."

I turn to look back at the car, my children's eager faces looking out of the window.

"Could we sit outside?" I ask. "On the balcony?"

The Cross-Section sits above the estuary and has far-reaching views across the water to the land on the other side, and out to sea. I really wouldn't mind sitting outside and enjoying the fresh air and those views.

"Isn't it a bit cold?" he asks doubtfully.

"We'll be fine," I say. "And we'd be happy with just some chips. Honestly. We just had to change our plans at the last minute."

He doesn't ask any more questions but calls over one of his waiters and asks him to take the covers off one of the outside tables, and to bring three chairs.

"If you get really cold, just come in. We'll work something out," says Christian.

"Thank you so much!" I say, and I go towards the car.

"Hi kids!" Christian calls. "I'm going to get you all a drink. Diet Cokes OK?" he asks me. He's well used to catering for people with a wide range of dietary needs and he gets it when it comes to diabetes. I'm very grateful.

"Perfect," I smile. "Thank you, I owe you one."

"No problem."

As it is, fortune smiles on us and the sun reveals itself, casting warm light directly onto the balcony and our seats. We still need our coats but it's warm enough. We order chips and garlic bread and the kids love crouching by the banister, watching the wading birds at the water's edge. I sit back and stretch my legs out in front of me, shielding my eyes against the sun. It feels like long-held tension is slowly leaking out of me, running through the cracks in the decking and dripping down into the muddy saltwater below; dispersing and drifting away. From inside the restaurant I can hear happy conversations and the soft notes of beautiful classical music while before me Ben and Holly laugh and chat, their backdrop a wide expanse of water and above them the bluest of skies.

It's a world away from the cabin fever that threatened this morning and I'm so glad we came out. We can eat, fill our tummies, head home to see Meg and watch a film, and then it's out again this evening to meet Sam (who will by then also have finished work for the next couple of weeks) and David, Martin, Esme and Tyler. We're eating out – again – with them and swapping presents before they head off north tomorrow. There will be no school to get ready for. No work to dictate our days. I sigh at the thought. It feels like Christmas has truly begun.

13

Ben, Holly and I are the first of our party to arrive at the Three Barrels; a lovely old building in a little village just outside town and on the road towards Amethi. It's been a pub for a long time but in recent years it's been taken over and upgraded to gastropub status; a destination pub, apparently. The owners have kept a side bar for the actual locals and in reality a lot of the people who do live locally are incomers like me.

I haven't been here for a while though, tending to avoid this side of town where possible. Too many memories; lovely memories but so lovely they make me feel sad. All those times zipping along the country lanes in the beaten-up red car Julie and I used to share. Whether I was heading to work or heading home, in those days when I lived in the cottage up there, I don't think there was ever a time that I didn't look forward to getting to Amethi. *Appreciate everything you've got*, I remind myself. Yeah, yeah. But I know it's true. And I do try.

The pub is low-ceilinged and hosts a welcoming fire at its heart. Our table is not too close to the fire, I'm pleased to see, because although it's lovely and very festive, today is mild and I fear that anyone sitting right next to the heat will soon be stripping off layers. I am, unusually, wearing a dress so I don't have layers to lose unless I want to sit in my underwear and I can't say I find that a very enticing prospect.

The lovely young waiter gives Holly and Ben Christmas-themed activity sheets and a fresh pack of colouring pencils each then leads the way to our table.

There is a 'Reserved for Branvall' sign propped up on the dark wood, accompanied by sprigs of holly and mistletoe. I still, even after all these years, love to see that name. *Sam Branvall.* I remember that delicious feeling the first time I saw those words displayed on my phone screen. The delight, the nerves, the sweaty palms and the anticipation as I opened the message. I don't remember what it said, which is telling; probably just something like 'Want to meet up later?' Young Sam wasn't much of a wordsmith. But that is all I'd have needed to send me head over heels.

Now, our messages are often practical. Reminders about school things; requests for an extra pint of milk or loaf of bread, or something the kids need for their homework or some kind of dressing-up day I'd forgotten about. Long gone are the sexier messages we used to send when we'd met up again in our late twenties. I feel like I'd be almost embarrassed to try and revive them. And somehow, these everyday messages mean more to me these days. They say we are a team. *We are in this together.* Maybe one day the romance will return, when we're older and the kids are older, and life is more simple again. But maybe we'll have missed the boat by then. Whatever will be will be. Just as long as we're together. I couldn't think of anybody I'd rather be sharing these familiar, dull messages with.

As if he knows I'm thinking about him, just as I'm helping Holly put her coat on the back of her chair, in walks my husband. Handsome as ever – to my eyes at least – he has come straight from work and he's wearing his blue jeans and a dark blue thick-knit jumper. His hair is slightly too long for his liking but I love it like this, and he's sporting a bit of a beard which just adds to his rugged, outdoorsy appearance.

"Alright?" he asks, kissing me and giving me an enquiring look.

"Yes, just thinking how gorgeous you are."

"Oh right, yeah, well you and everyone else in here." He clears his throat, slightly awkward despite his humour.

"Daddy! Daddy!" Holly saves him. "Help me find 'elf' in the word search."

"That's so easy," scoffs Ben.

"Ben," I say, "different people find different things easy. And you are two years older than Holly."

"Two and a half," he reminds me.

"Yes of course, two and a half." I ruffle his hair, grateful that he is a kind older brother most of the time. I'm aware as well that sometimes out of necessity Holly has more attention on her than he does. We do try to explain to him, and make sure we spend some one-on-one time with him once his sister's gone to bed but I wonder if it's difficult sometimes, having a sibling who has more pressing needs.

"Hello Branvalls, ho ho ho!" I hear and David bursts through the door followed by a very grown-up-looking Esme, who rolls her eyes, although I see she is grinning. Tyler and Martin follow on, leaving a metre of space so it might look like they're not with David.

"Hello!" I say, going across to hug and kiss them.

"Happy Christmas. Am I allowed to say that yet? It's not too early, is it?"

"It is exactly the right time, Alice my dear," says David. "Is that our table? Great. I'm starving. Have we got a tab?"

The tempo has changed as soon as David's stepped into the pub, and he tickles Holly so that she giggles, and goes to shake Ben's hand then pulls his own away and swipes it through his hair. Even Ben is not too cool to fall under David's spell. He's changed a lot over the years, my friend; initially my landlord, back then he had a lot going on emotionally. He and Bea, who was of course my boss in those days, had lost their parents in close succession and as a young man David had struggled with being gay and coming out, although when he did it wasn't as big a deal as he'd thought it would be. Still, he was a man with a bit of baggage, and then along came Martin and he helped take some of the weight away.

While I miss Julie and she will always be number one for me when it comes to friends, David comes a close second and I suppose it's like having a brother, making Martin a brother-in-law and Esme and Tyler my niece and nephew. It doesn't all need boxing up and labelling, of course. They don't need these titles; they are just people who I love. We all do, in fact.

"To all of us," I say, holding up my glass of water and feeling a bit overcome with emotion.

"Bit early for toasts though isn't it, Alice?" says David.

"It's never too early." Martin smiles kindly as he pulls his scarf loose then pours himself a glass of water. "I'll second that, Alice."

"Alright," David concedes and he and Sam hold their glasses up too.

All the children but Holly refrain. She shoots her plastic cup of squash into the air, sloshing it everywhere. "Cheers!" she says.

"Cheers, Holly." Martin gently knocks his glass against hers. "Now, are we having a real drink?"

I look at Sam. "We're both driving."

"You could leave your car here," he suggests. "I can drive you up to get it tomorrow. Go on, have a drink or two. Relax. You deserve it."

"Spoken like a true gent," says David. "Martin, you may have a drink as well. I shall drive our carriage then you can let your hair down. What you've got left of it."

Martin's hair could be described as, at best, receding. At worst, barely there. He just grins at David and picks up the wine list.

Esme sits next to Holly and helps her with all the puzzles, while Tyler gets his phone out and endures a lot of pleas from his parents until he can stand no more and puts it away again.

We are chatting so much that the waiter has to come back twice before we are able to order our food. I have already had two glasses of wine.

We order off the Christmas menu, which does make it a little bit easier, although Holly typically doesn't like the look of anything, so we have to order fish fingers and chips for her, and then Ben doesn't like the beetroot wellington that he ordered because Tyler did so we end up getting a second plate of fish fingers and chips. Pudding is a lot easier and we all have sticky toffee pudding and custard.

Even though we are a distance from the fire, I can feel my face growing flushed as the evening moves on.

"You're looking well there, Alice!" David says.

"Thanks," I say happily.

"Really," he moves his chair closer to mine, "it is nice to see you looking so happy. I've been a bit worried about you since, you know… Well, I don't want to bring the mood down. But I know how much you miss her."

"Thank you, David. It has been tough. But I really have to just give myself a talking to sometimes. It's not like anybody's died. And I am so incredibly lucky. I mean, look at them," I gesture slightly drunkenly to my family. "I just love them so much. And you guys. I love you too."

"That's the drink talking," David says mock sternly.

"It's not!" I protest, laughing. "You know it's not. Thank you, David, I hope Santa brings you everything you want."

"To be honest, Alice, don't tell Martin because he'll get a big head and we'll risk him losing even more of his follicles, but I think I've got everything I want."

"Bloody hell," I say, soberly. "Aren't we lucky?"

"We are," David says. "But do you know what? I think we deserve it." He pulls me into a hug and kisses my forehead. "Happy Christmas, Alice."

I switch to water soon after this exchange as I realise I'm a bit wobbly walking to and from the toilet. When we step outside into the stiff winter breeze which sweeps across the dark landscape, everything feels a bit surreal and I wish I'd had a coffee to help bring me back down to earth.

We hug each other goodbye and Martin and Sam surreptitiously exchange bags of presents. I go to the boot and see that their presents to us far outnumber ours to them.

"Bloody hell, where are we going to put all them?" I slur.

"Ssh!" says Sam. "Thank you," he says to David and Martin. "Have a brilliant Christmas. We'll see you for New Year's, won't we?"

"Are you at the Beach Bar, did you say? We'll drop by. But I have to warn you, we may not be there for long. And I doubt you'll see hide nor hair of Ty and Esme. They'll be off with their mates."

"Of course they will!" I smile at the pair of them in the back of David's car, heads already bent over phone screens, faces glowing ghostlike in the light. "Well, have a lovely Christmas, and give my love to your family won't you, Martin? And give Bea my love, David."

"We will," they chorus like a pair of schoolboys.

And then they're off, and then we are too. Now it really is just me, Sam, Ben, Holly and Meg. I feel pleasantly fuzzy as we leave the car park and I notice that tucked away at the far end is a mobile home. It makes me think of Mum and Dad's friend.

"I hope Nigel's made it to his niece's OK," I say to Sam.

"Who? Oh, the guy that turned up at your parents'? Poor bloke; his face when he realised they were going away for Christmas. He probably should have thought they might be busy, though."

"I know. I guess he just wanted to surprise them. They were very good to him, I suppose." I am so proud of my parents, that they're the kind of people who welcome somebody like Nigel into their home. Not that there's anything wrong with him – far from it – but often people get a bit wrapped up in themselves and don't want to risk inviting somebody else into their lives. A bit like I've been with Natalie, I suppose. My early new year's resolution is to do better. Be a better person. And stop moping around about missing Julie. I just have to accept she's gone. A second resolution is to make plans to visit her and Luke. It might mean pulling the children out of school for a week, which will be frowned upon, but I can't see how we could afford to do it in the school holidays.

I settle down in my seat, feeling quite drowsy in the heat of the car. Holly falls asleep on the way home and I feel like I could too. As soon as I've begun to relax, it seems that it's opened the flood gates for all of the fallout from the exhausted and exhausting days and nights. Of course it's possible the wine is adding to this but I really am tired. So very, very tired. And although I will miss our family and friends this Christmas, the thought of a few special days with just my husband, my children and our dog seems very enticing indeed.

14

When we get in, Sam can see how tired I am and, although he must be pretty shattered himself, he insists that I get an early night.

"If you want to, of course," he adds, not wishing to sound like he's bossing me about, but I'm already halfway up the stairs.

"I can think of nothing I'd like more," I reply and I am in the bedroom and pulling on my pyjamas before either of us has the chance to remember something I need to do.

After ten minutes or so I hear footsteps on the stairs and the familiar sounds of teeth-brushing and chatty voices – Holly woke up as soon as Sam put the handbrake on. I think the idea of Christmas and her birthday being imminent is keeping her little nerves on edge; in a good way of course, but she's practically jangling with nervous energy, Ben too. Consequently, this is a long and protracted bedtime and I feel a little bit guilty towards Sam for having to read the three – maybe four – bedtime stories and then sit with Holly while she falls asleep – and then go in to Ben and do the same with him. When they're like this if you leave them before they're fully out for the count they are guaranteed to get up within seconds of you exiting the room, supposedly needing a drink or one more story.

I must drift off before they do, because the next thing I'm aware of, and only dimly, is Sam's tread on the stairs, no doubt as he breathes a sigh of relief at being able to finally switch off, and then sometime later I feel him get into bed beside me and kiss me on the shoulder. He puts his arm across me and I can feel his breath on my neck, slowing down as he too falls asleep. In the warm darkness of the room, with the slight glow from the alarm clock, I feel safe and secure, and loved.

***

"Natalie! Let me in!"

Sam and I are both jolted awake by the shout, and we sit upright, looking at each other. I have an immediate horrible feeling in the pit of my stomach.

"Not again," says Sam, swinging his legs out of bed. "What are you doing?" he asks, seeing me getting out of the other side.

"I'm coming to see what's going on," I say. "And to make sure the children are OK." He can't argue with that. But really, I'm coming out with Sam. I'm not scared of Rob. Well maybe I am, a bit, but it's not going to stop me.

I peek in at Ben and Holly and thankfully they're both asleep. A quick check on my phone that Holly's blood sugars are OK. They're a little high, no doubt thanks to all the hefty carbs she ate at the pub and maybe her inner excitement too, but nothing to be concerned about.

I move quietly down the stairs as Sam is opening the front door. "Hang on," I say. "Wait for me."

We hear another shout from outside, and banging. Sam looks at me. I can tell he doesn't want me to come but he knows he can't order me to stay indoors. I pull my coat around me, zipping it up, and push my feet into my trainers. "Let's go," I say grimly.

I see curtains twitch at Jill and Raymond's window. They won't want to get involved. I do understand, they're getting on a bit and they also have to live next door to Natalie and Rob. It's awkward, but then what is a bit of awkwardness compared to putting a stop to this bullying behaviour?

"What's going on, Rob?" I say more confidently than I feel.

His head turns and he quickly recognises me, and Sam. "She won't let me in," he says, and I see immediately he's trying to sound reasonable. Trying to get me on side. "Hi mate," he says to Sam. "I'm sorry about the other night. I was just wound up, you know. She locked me out of the family home. You can understand I was pissed off. No hard feelings?"

Sam doesn't say anything.

"And you're locked out again," I say. "Do you know if Natalie's even in there?"

"She's in there, and she's changed the locks, the stupid… Well you know I took the kids out earlier, don't you, I saw you, and I brought them back, good as gold. We had a cup of tea, smoothed things over. You know it's not easy being married, is it?"

Neither Sam nor I speak this time. I want to hear what Rob's got to say. How he's going to try and weasel his way out of this one. I want to look at the house, work out if Natalie is really in there. And Bobby and Courtney. Are

111

they awake? Are they scared? I think of Ben and Holly. I don't like leaving them in the house without us, even though we are literally only metres away. But this whole situation has put me on edge. I shiver. Rob notices.

"Here, you're cold. Have my coat," he says, going to pull it off. I see it. The similarity to Geoff. The smooth, practised charm. So that people on the outside won't see the real him; just this shiny façade. The only thing is, he's slipped up this week, twice now.

"No, you're alright thanks," I say. "I'm fine."

He shrugs. Looks at Sam. "You get it mate, don't you? Life's hard sometimes. Work pressures, you know. She doesn't get it. She wouldn't, would she, looking after the kids and keeping the house nice? It's not exactly the same thing, is it?"

I look at Sam. I can see in his face he's trying to keep a lid on things. "It's not the same, no," Sam says, "but it's not any less or any more. And even if it was, it's not a reason to shout at your wife, or bang on your door and scare your children. What are you hoping to achieve?"

He speaks calmly and reasonably and I feel very proud of him.

"I know, I know, I shouldn't let it get to me," Rob says, trying out a penitent route. "But I'm tired, and I just want to go to bed. I'm sure we all do, don't we? I'm sorry if I disturbed you."

"Don't worry about us," says Sam, "but I think it's clear you won't be going to your bed tonight, don't you?"

"But it's my house. I pay for it." I can see the bubbles of anger starting to rise in Rob again.

I feel myself bristle. The classic argument about how he's the one going out to work. "And Natalie can't earn a wage,"

I say, "because she's looking after your kids – and *keeping the house nice*, like you said."

"I might have known you'd say that." He looks at me, the mask beginning to slip. "You 'work at home' don't you?" He's not so angry that he can't use air quotes when he says 'work at home'. "She's told me all about it. Wants to do the same. Just an excuse for sitting on your arse watching daytime TV, if you ask me."

My hackles rise and I feel Sam step closer to me. "I know Alice can answer for herself," he says, "but she works fucking hard at her job and then at doing everything else as well. If you ask me, it's me and you who've got the easy life."

"Easy?" Rob scoffs.

"Yeah. Easy. We get up, go out to work. Have a lunch break. Only have to think about ourselves. Alice gets up, has to get the kids ready for school, get them to school, come back, do a full day's work in about five hours, get the kids from school, deal with all the school shit, make them tea, and I get back just in time to do baths and bed. Which I love, by the way." He looks at me as he says this and I can't help but smile.

"Fair enough," Rob frowns. "So your missus actually works." He turns away now, done with us, and begins walking back to his front door. He bangs on it. "Natalie!" he shouts, then he opens the letterbox and his voice changes. "Just let me in, OK? Sorry. Sorry for shouting. I… oh Courtney, is that you? Hi Courtney, hi sweetie. Daddy forgot his key. Can you let me in…?"

"Oh no you don't," says Sam, and he rushes for Rob, grabbing him by the collar and swinging him back. "Sam!" I say, as Rob turns round, his face full of anger now.

I hear some fiddling behind the front door and I rush to it. "Just hang on Courtney, OK? Don't open the door," and I hear Natalie there as well, and I can hear Bobby crying. I place my hand on the door, wishing somehow to convey some comfort to them.

Rob swings for Sam and I'm terrified but then seemingly out of nowhere there are sirens and not one but two police cars rush into our street, sharp blue light slicing through the darkness, flashing and bouncing off windows, overwhelming the soft glow of the Christmas decorations.

Sam and Rob stand stock-still, and let go of each other. Sam puts his hands up, which would be funny if this wasn't such an awful situation.

The police exit their cars swiftly and move towards Sam and Rob, separating them and moving them both towards the cars. Shit, are they going to arrest Sam?

"It's that one," I hear, and I turn to see Raymond and Jill emerging from their house, Jill pulling the cord of her dressing gown tight as she shuffles outside in her slippers. Raymond is pointing to Rob. "He's the one causing the trouble."

"Alright sir, we'll assess the situation," says one of the police officers. "And we'll need to speak to all of you. Who called this in?"

"It was us," says Jill, timidly. "We're their next-door neighbours."

"And you are?" The police officer looks at me.

"I'm his wife," I gesture to Sam. "We just came out because we heard shouting. And it's not the first time."

"It's true," says Raymond.

"Alright, alright, what we're going to do is put you two–" the police officer points to Rob and Sam, directing colleagues – "in the cars, then we'll speak to you all separately."

Behind me, I hear the door open. I turn. "Natalie," I say, seeing her standing with Courtney in her arms and a sobbing Bobby clinging to her legs. "Are you OK?"

"I'm fine," she says brightly, clearly trying to keep a brave face on things for her children. "We're OK, aren't we kids? Daddy's just a bit cross, that's all."

How awful, having to try and reason with your children about this kind of thing. The police officer comes towards us. "Can you tell me who you are please?" she asks Natalie, who looks at me.

"Shall I take Bobby and Courtney to our house?" I ask. "We live three houses along, number 26," I tell the police officer. "And that's my husband your colleague has just put in the back of that car."

"OK." She seems to see the sense in this. "But I will need to speak to you."

"Thank you Alice," says Natalie, and I see she is shivering.

"No problem."

I usher the children along to our house and Meg seems to sense their distress. She plods up to us and even in this moment it makes these two children smile. I settle them on the sofa and go into the kitchen to make some hot chocolates, nipping up the stairs to check my own two kids are OK. And incredibly they are still sleeping on, dreaming and oblivious to the drama unfolding on their doorstep.

Downstairs, Bobby and Courtney are huddled next to each other. I tuck blankets around them. Meg curls up on the floor in front of where they're sitting, a guardian angel. I put the TV on and we select *Alvin and the Chipmunks* then

I go back to the kitchen and prepare some hot chocolates with cream and marshmallows. I am shaking too, and I feel cold, and I'm desperate to know what is unfolding outside. What if they do actually arrest Sam? But what would they arrest him for? I try to reason with myself but his black eye might not give the best impression.

Thankfully, I don't have to wait too long. While the children sip their hot chocolates, Courtney looking incredibly cute with a little blob of squirty cream on the end of her nose, I hear the front door and then I hear Sam's voice and then Natalie's.

"Alice?" I hear, said quietly.

"In here," I answer, and the two of them come in. "Shall we go into the kitchen?" I ask, and Sam nods.

"Come on," I say to Natalie, putting a hand on her arm. "So what happened? Did they arrest Rob?"

She shakes her head. "I didn't want them to. I can't very well press charges against my own husband, can I?"

Yes, I think, *you can*, but I know it's not as easy as that.

"And it's Christmas, isn't it?" I see tears spill from her eyes and I move to put her arms around her but she steps away. "Don't," she says. "I'm OK." And she visibly pulls her shoulders up. Takes a deep breath.

"Let's just have a cup of tea," says Sam. "I'd offer brandy if we had some."

"A shot of rum?" I suggest. "It'll take the edge off our nerves." Sam and Natalie look at me.

"Alright," says Sam. "Natalie?"

"Erm. OK. Just a little one."

And so the three of us have a quick shot of rum and as I feel the wave of warmth ripple through me Sam explains how Jill and Raymond told the police what had been happening and effectively got him off the hook, thanks also to Natalie telling her version of events. And the police had taken Rob with them down to town to go and sober up in the B&B he's been staying in.

"So you have chucked him out?" I ask, thinking that was perhaps not the most sensitive use of language.

"Yes." Natalie sniffs. "But he wanted to take the kids out today and I can't very well say no to that, can I? He brought them back earlier and we had a cup of tea and then he went down to town. Then he must have been drinking. At least he didn't drive up here. He'd be well over the limit."

"He shouldn't have been coming up here at all," I say grimly.

"He's upset though, isn't he?"

"I'm going to see if your two are OK, Natalie," Sam says. "I bet they're tired. Why don't you all just stay here tonight? You might relax better if you do. In the morning we can see what's what."

"Really?" Natalie's eyes shine with gratitude.

"Of course. It's no bother. I can make beds up for you all in the lounge. You can all be together."

I smile at Sam and wonder if it is possible to love someone more.

15

The two children are asleep within minutes and Sam says he's going to bed too.

I look at Natalie. "Want to talk?"

She nods. I wait.

Gradually she tells me her story, and I realise how little I knew about her. How for all those questions she asked me about myself and my family and my work, and Julie and Amethi, I must have barely asked her any about herself. In my defence she often didn't leave space for me to ask any questions in return, but still...

Natalie met Rob when she was a single mum, having split up with Bobby's dad before Bobby was even born. Rob was charming and handsome and seemed too good to be true. As it turned out, he was.

Natalie and Bobby had been living with Natalie's mum while Natalie saved up for a place for herself and her baby.

"I had a job that I loved, Alice. I was working for an events management company and it was really fun. A bit stressful but, you know, I really liked my colleagues, and it gave me a sense of achievement when things went well. And I was having driving lessons, and I thought it would be OK, just me and my little boy. But then Rob came along. He was one of our suppliers and he used to come and visit every month. I thought he was gorgeous. When he asked me out, I was so happy. You can't imagine."

I can imagine it only too well.

"Anyway, because he had to travel for work a lot I didn't really get to see him very often so he asked me to move in with him, he was living in Gloucester then, and I said yes but I felt bad for Mum, and I had to give up my job of course, but Rob said I'd find something else. And Mum really liked Rob. He fooled us both, I suppose. Then Rob asked me to marry him, and I found out I was pregnant, and everything moved so fast. I didn't get a chance to look for another job and Rob said nobody would take me on when I was pregnant anyway."

"Oh Natalie," I say sadly but I don't want to interrupt. It feels like she needs to tell her story.

"So there I was, in a place I didn't know, with no friends and no job, and Rob was away a lot with work. And when he was home he was stressed and not really very nice to be honest. His mum lives nearby and she'd come round a lot, but she wasn't very interested in Bobby and I don't think she really likes me. But she was happy I was pregnant, always going on about what a brilliant dad Rob was going to be to his real child."

"Oh Natalie. Poor Bobby. Poor you."

"I know. I'm an idiot. I should have turned round and left back then. But Courtney came along and she and Bobby took all my time. I hadn't carried on with driving lessons and Rob said I didn't need to. But Mum doesn't have a car and it was really difficult to see her. Rob was meant to drive us up every couple of months but we had to cancel so many times because something came up with him. Then he got this job down here."

"And now you're even further away from home," I say.

"Yes," she says sadly. "Though I do love it here. And the children really do."

"It is a lovely place," I say, "but I'm not sure that makes up for missing your mum."

I want to ask her what she'll do now but I know it's not as simple as that. She won't be able to make plans yet, she's only just beginning to process what's happened. There's even a chance that she'll have Rob back. I need to choose carefully what I say to her. I decide to tell her about Geoff.

So I go back over that painful time in my life, but I begin with meeting Sam that long-ago summer, and that makes her smile, but as I progress the story and tell her about my own awful relationship with a controlling partner, I see her eyes glisten with tears but I'm not looking for her sympathy. I just want her to know that I know. When I get close to the end of the story, I question whether to tell her what happened to Geoff. It may be too much for tonight.

I am saved by Courtney, who wakes and wonders where she is. "Mummy?" she calls.

"I'm here, darling."

"Go on through, Natalie," I say.

"But you were saying…"

"Don't worry about it," I smile. "I'm just grateful you told me your story. Thank you."

We hug briefly then she goes through to cuddle her daughter. I head upstairs to get some extra blankets for Natalie and when I come back she's tucked in between Bobby and Courtney on the makeshift bed that Sam has constructed from chair and sofa cushions.

She smiles at me. I lay the blankets across her and blow her a kiss. "Sleep well."

"Thank you, Alice."

Sam murmurs as I go into the bedroom. I pad across to the window and look out into the darkness. It's Christmas Eve but right now it couldn't feel less like it. My mind flicks through memories of Christmas Eves past and how thrilling it felt when I was little. I want it to be like that for Ben and Holly, and for Bobby and Courtney, while they're still young enough to really believe in magic.

16

Christmas Eve morning is beautiful. I open the curtains to see the sky is a light winter blue, with very thin strands of clouds pulled across it like cotton wool stretched to breaking point.

Holly had come into our bed at some point during the early hours and wriggled her way down between me and Sam. As the morning light began to creep into our room I snuggled my face against her warm, soft pyjamas and felt her morning breath on my cheek.

"Are you awake, Mummy?" Holly's attempts at whispering were so poor that I could only conclude she was not really trying to whisper.

"Mmmmm," I said.

"There's people downstairs."

"What? Oh yes, there are. It's Courtney and Bobby and their mummy."

"What are they doing here? Is it a surprise?"

Fully awake, I had put my arms around Holly. "They had a bit of a tricky night last night."

"Why?"

This was a tough one. I decided to go with a watered-down version of events; after all, Bobby and Courtney had both witnessed their dad's behaviour so there was a good chance they might mention it to my two anyway.

"Natalie and Rob had a bit of an argument and I invited Courtney and Bobby and Natalie in for a hot chocolate, then they got really tired so I said they should just stay here."

"Like when you get cross with Daddy?"

"No not really. I don't get cross with Daddy, do I?"

"Sometimes."

"But… well I suppose that's normal when you live with people. Sometimes you get cross with your family when it's not really them you're annoyed at."

"Why?"

"That's a good question." I was really having to work at cranking my over-tired brain into action. "I suppose it's because they're the closest people to you and you know that you can get cross sometimes but it's OK. You feel safe with them."

Holly started fidgeting, bored of the conversation and eager to see her friends. I saw Sam stirring next to her as well.

"Come on," I said. "Let's get the curtains open, see what kind of day Christmas Eve is going to be!" And we've been rewarded with this beautiful sight which greets me now.

"Beach day!" I say jokingly.

"Yes!" Holly punches the air.

"Sorry Holly, I think it might be a bit cold really," I tell her gently. "But we could go for a walk on the beach, couldn't we Sam? Before we go and collect my car from the pub? And then this afternoon we're going to Paul and Shona's."

"Yay!" Holly bounces on the bed and suddenly Ben is there, landing on Sam with a painful thud.

"Urgh, Ben, watch where you land!" Sam curls up to protect himself. Ben has lost all need to appear cool, it seems, in the face of all this excitement.

"It's Christmas Eve!" he says.

"And birthday eve!" shouts Holly. "And Bobby and Courtney are downstairs."

"No they're not," Ben says.

"They are Ben, they stayed over last night."

"Is that why all those pillows and blankets are down there?"

"Yes, have you been down already?"

"I went to get a drink," he says and it sounds pathetic because he's eight so of course he's capable of getting his own drinks, but it just strikes me how grown up he's getting.

"So you saw Bobby?"

"There's nobody there, Mum," Ben says, and he does actually sound like a teenager. I experience a vision of the eye-rolling which is sure to come.

"Really?" I get out of bed and pull on a jumper then I head downstairs, Holly hot on my heels. She is disappointed to see that our guests have gone, replaced by neatly folded duvets and blankets and a small pile of pillows. I'm reminded of the closing scene of *The Snowman* when – sorry if this is a plot-spoiler – James rushes out to see his friend to find just a hat, scarf and some lumps of coal lying on the snow.

I hope Natalie is alright, and the children too. I'd have liked to have seen them and made them all some breakfast. I open the curtains and see there is a note on the table.

Dear Alice and Sam,

Thank you so much for your kindness last night. We don't want to get in the way and I'm going to try and work out if we can get to my mum's for Christmas so we're going home now. Don't think us rude for just leaving, please. We hope you have a lovely Christmas and that Holly has a very happy birthday. Love Natalie, Bobby & Courtney xxx

It's a relief in a way I suppose as I don't know what we'd have done today if they had wanted to stay longer. Still, if they're going up to see her mum that will be good for her, and for Bobby and Courtney too.

I send a quick WhatsApp:

I hope you make it to your mum's OK and that you can have a happy Christmas. Looking forward to seeing you when you get back xx

"Pancakes?" I ask Holly, feeling the need to bring some festive focus to the morning.

"Yes!" she says, shouting, "Ben! Pancakes!"

He comes whizzing down the stairs only to be disappointed when he realises that there are no pancakes as yet; just a bag of flour, some eggs and some milk. Then his face brightens with an idea. "Can I make them, Mum?"

"Let's do it together, shall we?" I suggest tactfully, not sure he's quite ready for solo pancake-making yet.

So we pull up the step for him to reach the counter, and Sam comes downstairs, putting on the radio and then picking up Holly and dancing her around the room to *Rockin' Around the Christmas Tree*. It's a scene fit for a schmaltzy made-for-TV movie. But it's lovely.

We eat our pancakes with lemon juice and sugar, or chocolate spread, drinking orange juice – and coffee for the grown-ups. Meg has a pancake and I'm happy to see she wolfs it down.

"Think she's up to a walk on the beach?" I ask Sam.

"I don't see why not."

So we get dressed and bundled up in warm coats, and I load the car with wellies for the kids and then get the ramp so Meg can get in the boot. She used to just jump in with ease.

"We're all getting older Meg," I say, and she licks my face.

Then we're off! Down to the surfing beach where the open aspect allows the wind to beat and buffet us, and blow sand in our faces. There are surfers on the waves, of course – there are some who will be there whatever the time of year – and there are of course other dog-walkers and families enjoying the bright daylight and trying to work off some of the nervous energy in the face of the big day.

Meg is slow but happy to be on the beach, lifting her face to take in the smells. We go at her pace and the children are more than happy running in and out of the waves bare-foot. I don't know why I bothered packing wellies.

The Beach Bar is open so we stop by for a hot chocolate for the kids and a further coffee for me and Sam.

Andrew and Becky aren't there today so we chat to Star, their second-in-command. Holly is in awe of Star, who is in her late twenties and has a pierced lip, a tattoo that winds its way up from her spine onto the nape of her neck, and bright red hair. When she's not working at the Beach Bar, Star is often one of those people out on their boards on the waves or running yoga-on-the-beach classes during the warmer months. I feel like she and Lizzie would get on well.

Then it's back to the car, where we have to coax a very tired Meg up the ramp, and back home. The day, which had at first light seemed to stretch luxuriously before us, is already rushing along, and we're due at Paul and Shona's in a couple of hours. We need to collect my car from the Three Barrels car park and we also still need to have lunch and get showered and changed.

"Don't stress about it!" Sam says. "It's just Paul and Shona."

But I do feel a little bit stressed. Yes, they're our friends, but Shona is also now my boss. And – though I'd never suggest to Sam that this matters – Paul is my ex. They're both so gorgeous and well put together, and their house so upmarket and spotless, I feel like I need to polish myself as well as I possibly can for them.

I have a few minutes to myself when I'm driving my car home from the Three Barrels and I practise my slow, deep breathing. This is not meant to be a stressful day, and by and large it isn't. But I do wish that we just had a nice afternoon at home before us, rather than a social engagement. Still, I've been complaining that we will miss people over Christmas so I really should be looking forward to socialising. Why do I always want things both ways?

When I get back, Sam opens the front door for me, to reveal a scene of carnage. There are those little white polystyrene packing peanuts all over the hallway floor and two children sitting amongst them, tossing them into the air over each other's heads and laughing.

"It's snowing, Mummy!" Holly giggles.

"What's all this?"

"We got a gift," Sam says. "From your famous friends."

"My…?"

"Well, one's famous anyway."

"Not Lydia and Si?" I step forward and see that just inside the lounge doorway is a huge hamper, which clearly the children have already made a start on unpacking. Sam has sensibly put the glass bottles up on a table but still in the case, and placed on the floor around it are what seem to be endless goodies. I see cheeses, chocolates, crackers, fruit jellies, fudge, butter, apple juice, orange juice, wine, champagne, olives, sweet biscuits, jars of pickle and jam and honey… even dog biscuits and a huge chew with a bow wrapped round it.

"Oh my god!" I laugh.

"I know. There's a card as well."

I take it from Sam's hand and read:

Merry Christmas Alice, Sam, Ben, Holly and Meg. By the time you read this we will be sunning ourselves on our own private decking and it won't feel like Christmas at all. But we hope you guys have a wonderful family time and that these little treats help you do so. Much love, L & S xxxx

"Little treats!" I laugh.

"I know. If I'd known this was coming I wouldn't have bothered with that Tesco shop!"

"This is so lovely though." I think of Shona spilling the beans on Lydia's pregnancy and imagine that Lydia was looking forward to their own wonderful family Christmas next year when she composed that message. I will keep everything crossed for her that all goes well with the pregnancy. She is young and fit and healthy so she has everything on her side – as well as access to Si's private medical professionals, I would imagine. I'm so happy for her.

"Are you crying?" asks Sam.

"What? No," I say, discreetly wiping a single tear from my cheek. I just remember what it's like knowing that you're pregnant for the first time but I can't say that to Sam without telling him Lydia's news. "It's a happy tear," I say.

"Good." Sam puts his arms round me. "But kids, I hate to break up your party but we need to clear this all up. We don't want Meg eating any of those polystyrene Wotsits, do we? Or Mummy, for that matter."

That makes them laugh and I am relieved that they join in the clearing-up operation in good spirits. We shovel all the packaging into a plastic bag, which Sam ties up and takes straight out to the garage. I'm sure we'll find some use for them somewhere along the line.

Then we carry all our goodies through to the kitchen and I try to find homes for them all but end up giving up and piling them on the work surfaces. We really do have to go soon, we can sort this out later.

While I'm getting ready I hear my phone ping. It's Natalie.

Thank you Alice, we're all OK. I don't know if we will get to Mum's. It's a long way and lots of changes, and you know what trains are like at Christmas. So we might just stay here x

I just hope that Rob steers clear from now on. Hopefully with the police involvement, he might have been a bit scared off. But I know as well as anyone that these things don't always just end cleanly, and I also know that they don't stop for Christmas.

OK, well if you change your mind and you need a lift to the station, or anything at all, let me know x

Even as I send that I wonder how I'd be able to give her a lift to the station when I'll be at Paul and Shona's but after months of being a, frankly, crap friend, I'm eager not to be any longer.

Thank you x

And that's that for now. What else can I do? Natalie knows I'm willing to help if I can. *Let me know if I can do anything.* Those words pop into my head. Am I effectively doing that? But no, it's Christmas, and we are busy, and we did help her out last night. I will check in on her later though. For now, I have to shower and choose some clothes. It's telling that I go through five different outfits; Sam comes in at number three to get changed, which takes him all of two minutes, and rolls his eyes as he sees me turning this way and that in front of the mirror.

"Not hoping to win Paul back are we?" he grins, but I feel annoyed.

"No of course not!" I say then I blush and admit, "If I'm trying to impress anyone it's Shona. She's so bloody effortlessly... glam."

"Alice," Sam approaches me and puts his hands lightly on my shoulders then turns me round to face him. "A) it is probably far from effortless for Shona to look how she does and B) you are just beautiful as you are. Don't give me that look. You are. You don't need to worry like this about what you look like, what you're wearing…"

"But I want to feel confident," I protest.

"Yes but as you always say to Holly and Ben, it shouldn't be what you look like that matters. Your clothes don't mean anything. I heard you say that to Ben when he was talking about George's flash Nikes or whatever."

"I know," I say, kissing him. "But I'm just going to try one more thing on."

"I give up!" he laughs. "Just let me know when you're ready."

"I won't be long, I promise!"

***

Although it is only early afternoon when we arrive at Paul and Shona's, the day is beginning to feel dark. Those promising early clear skies have gradually been hidden away by a thick layer of grey cloud, which doesn't feel Christmassy. It does, however, mean that the lights hanging in the trees around the garden and along the balcony railings get the chance to really shine.

"I love this place!" says Ben. "And Paul's cars!"

"Yeah," says Sam, "it is all pretty special."

I glance at him to see if there is an edge of sarcasm or disapproval but I think he actually means it. He's not the jealous sort. I take his hand. Sam looks at me and smiles.

Holly runs to the door, which is flung open by Shona.

"Welcome!" she says. "Hi Holly!" She crouches down and Holly flings herself into her arms, which makes Shona laugh. It's always good to see her in a non-work setting and remember what a lovely, warm person she is.

"Come in, come in," she says, hugging me and kissing Sam on the cheek, then shaking Ben's hand solemnly. "Quite the young man now, Ben," she says and he blushes. She may be at least fifty years his senior but he's not immune to her charms.

Paul, wearing immaculate designer jeans and a hoodie, appears in the hallway as we walk in. "Hi you guys!" he says and I think that he's trying very hard to stay young.

"Hello Paul." I smile and hug him. He kisses me on the cheek and I can smell his expensive aftershave, then he steps back to shake Sam's hand and greet Holly and Ben, who are quite shy with him. Although he is a dad and Shona has no children of her own, it seems that she is more of a natural with them.

"Let me take your coats," Paul says, "and come on through to the living room."

The house looks incredible; there are little clusters of fairy lights above mirrors and pictures, and in the living room is an absolutely huge Christmas tree, the tip of which reaches all the way up to the mezzanine balconies above.

"How on earth did you get that in here?" I ask.

"You don't want to know," Shona laughs. "Let's just say it wasn't pretty, and it wasn't cheap."

"Bit over the top, if you ask me." An older man who I assume is Shona's dad – largely due to his Scottish accent – stands up to greet us. "I'm Malcolm."

"Dad, this is Alice who I work with, and her husband Sam, and these two are Ben and Holly."

I notice how quiet my children have become.

"Grand to meet you all," Malcolm says.

"And over there," Shona gestures to an even older man, "is Derek, Paul's dad. *He's a bit hard of hearing,*" she

132

whispers so I smile at Derek and move towards him but not before I hear Malcolm say, "Which makes it easier to wind him up."

"Dad!" Shona says warningly.

"Don't stand," I say to Derek as I see him struggling to do so. I hold out my hand. "Pleased to meet you. I'm Alice."

"Alex? Strange name for a woman."

"A-liss," I enunciate, thinking that actually Alex is a perfectly fine name for a woman anyway.

"Oh, *you're* Alice," he says, "I've heard a lot about you." That surprises me. From Paul or Shona? "Nice to meet you. Sit yourself down, I'm sure my son will get you a drink. Paul!" he barks and Paul appears from the kitchen.

"Yes, Dad?"

"Get Alice a drink!"

"That's what I'm doing," says Paul, disgruntled, and it makes me smile to see that even Paul Winters is not above regressing to becoming an irritated son.

In time, he brings through a tray with champagne flutes and bowls of pistachios and cashews. Then he returns with a bottle of champagne which looks to have been chilled to perfection, and a glass bottle of orange juice. From his pockets he produces Fruit Shoots and bags of crisps.

"I'd prefer them," Derek says to me in what he thinks is a quiet voice but which everyone else can clearly hear.

"Well I'd love some champagne," I say, and Paul smiles at me gratefully. "But just a small glass because I'm driving. Maybe we could make it a Bucks Fizz?"

"That's a shame," says Paul.

"I drank last night," I explain then hasten to add, "not that we take it in turns. I mean, we don't drink every night..."

Malcolm laughs. "Methinks the lady doth protest too much."

Shona shoots me a look from over his shoulder. "Anyway, I'll give Georgia and Lenny a shout, I know they'd like to say hello."

"Spend too much time on their phones," Derek mutters.

"They're fine, Dad," Paul snaps. I'm beginning to remember why family Christmases aren't always what they're cracked up to be.

"Go and get them, Paul," Shona suggests gently and he takes her hint gratefully. I feel like they both might need to have the other's back over the next couple of days.

It's been some time since I've seen Paul's children and really, children isn't the word for them these days. They are well into their twenties, both lovely and grown-up and chatty and brimming with confidence. It makes me miss Sophie; she's not that much younger than these two. Georgia's boyfriend is a lovely young man called Samir and just the fact I have referred to him as a lovely young man makes me feel old. He's training to be a doctor and I can see Paul very much approves of him.

Lenny's girlfriend, on the other hand, tells us she is carving out a career as an influencer and I glance at Paul, knowing full well what he will think of this. Malcolm suppresses a laugh and Derek utters, "She's explained to me countless times and I still have no idea what she's talking about."

Only Shona seems to think it could be a good thing; "Letitia's got a great following on Insta and TikTok, and I was thinking maybe she could talk to you in the new year, Alice. Maybe we can get her some promo work."

"Sure," I smile at Letitia. She is flawlessly beautiful, and even in my carefully selected clothes I feel old and shabby in comparison. But as we get chatting I realise she's really nice, and she's also clearly intelligent. She does have another job, working for an IT company, which sounds quite complex but she says is boring. "That's why I tell people I'm an influencer," she explains. "I'm trying to manifest it."

"I think that's good." I end up telling her about Amethi and how Julie and I had wanted to run our own business for years before we made it happen.

"Is this the place Si Davey has now?" Letitia asks.

"Yes," I say.

"That's a shame, that you don't do it anymore."

"It is," I agree, "but life moves on. You know… family… kids…"

She nods but I know she doesn't really get it. Why should she?

It's a lovely afternoon and we are made to feel very welcome but after a couple of hours I can sense the children are at the far end of their supply of patience. Everyone is lovely to them but there isn't a lot to do and I think even they can sense that this is not a place to mess around in. All drinks must be on coasters, and crumbs are sucked up – albeit apologetically – almost instantaneously by Shona with her tiny hand-held hoover.

I have spoken at length with Derek about the book of coastal walks he is compiling although he is hampered, he says, by the fact he can't get out and actually do the walks these days. "So it's all from up here," he says, tapping his head. "Keeps the mind sharp, though."

Malcolm had chuckled quietly when he heard those words. I am not sure I've taken to Shona's dad to be honest, and I can see why Shona was keen to dilute the atmosphere with a few more guests. But we can't stay longer just to make life easier for her. I say my goodbyes to the dads, and to Georgia, Lenny, Samir and Letitia, who have taken their party out onto the darkening decking. I can't say I blame them.

"Thanks for coming," Shona says.

"Thanks for inviting us. I'm just wondering where Sam and Paul have got to."

Where they've got to, as it turns out, is one of Paul's fancy cars. Sam is sitting in the driver's seat, Paul in the passenger seat, and between them is a bottle of champagne. The radio is on loud and there is a lot of laughter coming from the car.

"You know, I don't think it's Paul's feelings for you I need to worry about. I think it's your husband he's got a crush on!" Shona laughs then says, "Sorry, that was really inappropriate. I don't really worry about him having feelings for you."

"I should hope not!" I laugh too, though it is a bit awkward in honesty. This is what happens, I think, when you're the only one not drinking. "You two are perfect for each other. But you're right, I do sense a bit of a bromance developing."

I knock on the window and Sam jumps. Then he and Paul collapse into more laughter. It makes me smile. "Come on, time to go," I say as Sam opens his window. I call to Ben and Holly, who are currently running round and round the trees, chasing each other and wearing off some of their excess energy.

"Oh, I almost forgot!" says Shona. "Wait there!" And she vanishes into the house, returning with her arms full of gift bags. "Just some little things for the kids. And for Holly's birthday," she tries to whisper. I feel like she's about as effective as her father-in-law.

"My birthday!" Holly shouts. "And Christmas!" Ben throws a handful of leaves into the air and they both cheer then lose themselves in giggles. "You're as bad as your dad," I say, and apologise to Shona for any excess mess in a garden which is almost as pristine as the house.

"Ach it's no bother," she says, but I could swear her eyes are roving the lawn looking for any divots or skids from the children's running around. Definitely time to go.

"Thank you so much," I say, opening the car boot and feeling guilty that all Shona's beautifully packaged gifts are going straight onto Meg's blanket, which is coated in sand and dog hair. "But you already gave me that bonus," I say quietly.

"Yes well that was a work thing and this is a friends thing." She hugs and kisses me. "I think the world of you, Alice. I hope you have a lovely Christmas."

I return her hug. "Thank you Shona, really."

And as I climb into the driver's seat, my passengers all excitable and giggly, including Sam, the unpleasant chill of last night seems to have vanished. I'm glad now that we came out; it's put a bit of space between us and the recent drama and brought us back round to Christmas. Even so, after I pull up onto our drive, while Sam takes Ben and Holly indoors I wander along to Natalie's house. I don't want to knock and disturb her; it is Christmas Eve after all, but I do want to make sure everything looks OK.

As it is, the lights are off, the curtains closed, and I'm glad to see there is no car in the driveway. I guess they have gone up to her mum's after all. I'm sure it will do them all good. And I'm hopeful we'll get a good night's sleep tonight. At least until the kids wake us up at about half past three…

17

When I step through our front door I am greeted by Meg, who seems relatively frisky, no doubt carried along on the wave of Ben and Holly's excitement. The children have already got into their Christmas pyjamas and they rush to me as I come in.

"You got changed quickly!" I say.

"We're getting ready," Ben explains, "so we can go to bed early and then it'll be Christmas quicker."

"I like your thinking," I say, and I'm pleased he lets me hug and kiss him. He may not like public displays of affection but he's not too old to have a cuddle with me at home. Long may it continue.

"So what do we need to do?" I ask, thinking I wouldn't mind going to bed early myself.

"Stockings!" shouts Holly, waving hers around.

"Careful, you'll have someone's eye out!" I laugh.

"I won't." Holly looks doubtful.

"No, not really. But be careful!"

"It's just a sock, Mum," Ben scoffs.

"Well, anyway…" I say, not wanting to get into a debate over whether you can hurt somebody with an empty sock,

"Where are we putting them? In your rooms or outside your doors?"

"Outside," Holly says. She's been put off the idea of having a stocking in her bedroom by Ben, who used to be terrified by the idea of Father Christmas actually coming into his room while he was asleep. Which really is very sensible, to be honest.

"I'm having mine on the end of my bed," Ben says grandly and Holly looks at him admiringly. I imagine Janie used to look at Sam that way. There is an even bigger age gap between the two of them. I bet he seemed like an absolute hero to her. In some ways I think he still does.

"OK," I smile. "Let's go and see where you want them, shall we?" And I follow the two of them upstairs, loving their energy and their sweet excitement. I would like to prolong their childish innocence for as long as I can because once you've begun to make that approach on adulthood there is no going back.

Holly decides to lay her stocking flat on the floor outside her door, and Ben plays about with his, deciding that actually he might not have it on his bed: "It might fall off and Father Christmas might not find it. I'll just leave it here next to the door so he only has to come in a little way."

"Very sensible," I say.

And then it's off back downstairs and into the kitchen, where Sam has got out a bag of carrots and a box of mince pies. We smile at each other. How is it possible not to love Christmas?

Ben and Holly busy themselves arranging the carrot and pie on a plate, and then Holly decides to get one of Meg's food bowls for the carrot, and Ben pours a careful glass of milk.

"I thought we normally left some whisky for Santa?" Sam asks.

"Honestly Dad, he can't have so much whisky if he's driving, can he?" Ben reasons. "And milk is nice."

There's no arguing with this logic so milk it is.

While they are deciding where to place the plate, milk and dog bowl, I begin to warm some more milk for hot chocolates, and I put the kettle on. Boring though it may sound, I just fancy a cup of tea.

"What's next?" Sam asks Ben and Holly.

"Snowman!"

"Of course. I'll go and get it lined up," Sam says. "Shout if you need a hand, Alice."

I do hot chocolates with the works for Ben and Holly, a cup of ginger tea for myself, and 'normal' tea for Sam. I barely drink normal tea these days and think wistfully of those mixes that Lizzie used to make, for solstices and other special occasions. I'd love to know how to do that properly but my attempts to date have been pretty disappointing.

I take the tray through and return to the kitchen for a selection box of biscuits. With our drinks and snacks on the coffee table, the four of us manage to squeeze onto the settee and then Ben gets up to switch off the lights so it's just the Christmas tree that fills the room with its cosy illumination. As the music from *The Snowman* filters into the room I close my eyes and just think about how lucky I am.

"Are you OK, Alice?" Damn, Sam has noticed.

"Yes I am," I smile, opening my eyes. "More than OK. Happy Christmas, all of you."

"Happy Christmas Mummy," says Holly and I'm gifted a proper, full-on cuddle from Ben. It feels very good.

After *The Snowman*, the children decide they're ready for bed. It's not even eight yet so this bodes well. I take Ben and Sam takes Holly and it's not long at all before they drop off. I had thought that we'd be trying to calm them down forever. I think that, had they had a 'sleepover' in Ben's room as they had initially wanted to, this could have been a very different story.

For a while, I watch Ben sleep. Stroking his hair gently back, I see a succession of all the Bens I've known over the years, in that familiar shape of his head; the high forehead and the round cheeks, which are still soft and squidgy but won't be forever. I try to picture all the Bens which are yet to come. A wave of love travels through me, for how this little person has changed my life and changed me. And now he's growing up, as he must and he should. But he and Holly have made my life about them, about being a mum, yet the day will come when they move on and up and out into the world, and life will change again. It's a strange thought and I know it's a long way off but doesn't everybody say these years fly by? How many more till Ben doesn't believe in Father Christmas anymore? I look at the stocking laid on the floor, just inside the door. This is already a change. Is it a sign that he already doesn't quite believe as he did, or just that he is just growing older and braver? I kiss his forehead and dim his lamp then stand up and make my way quietly to the door, opening it to see Sam has just emerged from Holly's room.

We look at each other and, it seems, are both suddenly filled with a rush of Christmas excitement. Sam grins at me and I have to try very hard not to giggle.

"Ssh!" Sam says, in an exaggerated whisper and he leads the way downstairs, tiptoeing in an over-the-top way.

At the bottom, he waits for me and takes my hand. "My lady," he says.

"Thank you, good sir."

And suddenly we are kissing, in a way that we haven't in a long time. I feel his hands on my waist, and the warm familiarity of his mouth on mine.

"Steady on," I say, pulling back for a moment, aware of all the things we still have to do. "Don't you know it's Christmas?"

"I just love you," he says into my hair. "So much. And I want you."

I feel a little churning of excitement somewhere deep within, but this is not for now. I know it, and Sam knows it. We look at each other.

"Presents?" he says, resignedly.

"Presents," I agree.

"Where do we start?"

"I don't even know. They're everywhere."

"Tell you what, I'll get the ones in from the car, from today. You start getting the ones we've hidden downstairs, just in case those two aren't in quite as deep a sleep as we'd like."

"Good plan," I say and Sam moves to pick up the keys but I take his hand, pull him back to me and kiss him. I look into his eyes. "I love you too, Sam."

"But do you want me?" He looks back at me, and I think of all the times his eyes have been on mine. How I used to get flustered, and look away, back when we were young and had first got together.

"I do," I say, and I kiss him again, lingeringly. He returns my kiss but this time it's Sam who pulls back.

"It's all about the timing," he smiles. "We've got lots of

days off this year. Let's make at least one of them about us, shall we? When your folks are back. Maybe they'll have the kids and we can have some time together."

"I would love that." It may not be very spontaneous planning our time this way but I still find it romantic. "But for now… presents."

We gather the various sets of presents together in the lounge, and I really hope that neither of the children wake up now. I'm on edge, keeping half an ear out for them and another half for any noises in the street. We could definitely do without another night of drama from Rob.

As the piles grow higher, I begin to think it is ridiculous. We have the presents we've bought from us, the presents from Father Christmas, from Mum and Dad, from Karen and Ron, from Julie and Luke, David and Martin, Shona and Paul… there are gifts from neighbours and work friends, and then there are also Holly's birthday presents.

"I actually feel a little bit sick, looking at all of these."

"I know what you mean," says Sam.

"It's way too much."

We spend some time looking at all the shiny parcels and bags.

"I blame our parents," I say, but I'm smiling.

"They can't help themselves, can they?"

"What if–" I say, thinking this through – "we put away the presents from Mum and Dad? At least until after lunch. Or else they can give them to Ben and Holly themselves, when they're back. And maybe we suggest to Holly that she has her birthday presents on Boxing Day? Or even the day after, when she's had her party." I have no idea how that will go down with Holly but it's got to be worth a go.

"OK," Sam says, thinking this through. "Good plan."

So it's back to the bedroom with Mum and Dad's gifts, where I push them gently under our bed, while Sam piles Holly's birthday presents back into the cupboards. Even when this is done, there's still such an excessive heap of gifts in the lounge. Still, as we begin to place them under the tree, the fairy lights making the fancy paper twinkle, it does look enchanting. For Ben and Holly to come downstairs in the morning and think Santa has been... maybe it's not so bad.

We stand back and admire our work. Sam puts his arm round me and I lean against him. "I'm so tired."

"Me too."

It seems inconceivable that just an hour or so ago we were kissing enthusiastically at the bottom of the stairs. Where had that energy come from? Maybe more importantly, where has it gone?

"Shall we go up?" I ask. I do love Christmas Eve and in previous years it's been lovely sitting up with Sam watching a film and just unwinding but I have learned from experience now that going to bed at midnight might mean just three hours' sleep. I don't think I can cope with that this year, on top of the other disturbed nights we've been having.

"That sounds good," Sam admits.

"Happy Christmas, my love," I say, turning and kissing him, and he kisses me back and then hugs me. I press my face against his chest and breathe in, feeling all the warmth and strength of the man I married.

And then it's back to business. Christmas is coming. We must remember to change the stockings. It would not do to forget to switch the empty ones for the pre-prepared versions. I'm grateful for our unusual forethought and organisation in getting them done in advance this year. But it's going to be a bit trickier now that Ben's laid his empty stocking inside his room. I'm just grateful it's not on his bed.

We switch off lights and I let Meg out for a night-time wee and Sam waits so that we head upstairs together, hand in hand. I think of our lucky children, safe in their warm beds, all the excitement of Christmas yet to come.

And then, as we reach the landing, I see that Ben, growing up though he may be, has clearly woken enough to have a change of heart. His empty stocking lies rumpled just outside his bedroom door.

18

"It's Chriiiiistmas!"

"Birthday!"

"Christmas!"

"Birthday!"

"Christmas!"

"Birthday Christmas!"

There is an explosion of laughter from Ben and Holly. I turn to look at my clock. Only 5.14 am. It could be worse.

"Come here you two," Sam says, and up they clamber, sharp knees and elbows finding all the wrong places.

"Ouch!" I laugh. "Come on, get under the covers. Did you bring your stockings?"

"Yes," says Ben.

"I forgot mine," wails Holly.

"I'll get it." Ben scoots off the bed and out of the door and he is back within moments, holding Holly's stocking triumphantly.

"Well done Ben," says Sam.

"Thank you Ben," Holly says sweetly.

"Erm, Holly…" I say.

"Yes?"

"Happy birthday!" I roll her onto her back and blow raspberries on her tummy so that she squeals. I stop and look down at her. "How does it feel to be six?"

"It's funny."

"Well that's good." I watch Ben, who is sitting at the tail end of the bed, feeling his stocking, the wrapped paper packages crackling and crunching satisfyingly inside their soft woollen home. "Ben?"

"Yes?"

"Happy Christmas!" I launch myself at him, giving him the same treatment I had Holly. He belly-laughs until he realises he really is too old for this now. "Stop, Mum," he says breathlessly.

"Sorry, I'm just a bit over excited."

Ben ruffles my head affectionately like I'm the child. I have a brief glimpse of the future.

"What are you waiting for?" Sam asks, evidently a bit excited himself. "Come on, I want to see what Father Christmas has brought you."

I look at him. He's so convincing I half believe he really doesn't know that we bought and wrapped all the stocking fillers ourselves.

"What?" he asks, hands held high.

And we sit back and exclaim and laugh and admire the items our children hold up, their unwrapping becoming increasingly frantic, until our bed is covered in chocolate coins and mini soaps, shampoos and body washes, while the clockwork toys race each other across Sam's bedside table, and Holly is pulling on her new socks, but onto her hands instead of her feet.

"Is that everything?" asks Sam.

"Yes," Holly looks momentarily disappointed but her

face quickly brightens. "Can we go downstairs now?"

"Not yet," I say. "It's only quarter to six." I groan inwardly. Half an hour in and the stockings are already done and dusted. "Coffee?" I ask Sam.

"I'll get it," he says. "Although there is one more thing. I think Father Christmas left this for your mum," he says to Ben and Holly. They look amazed at the beautiful little gift bag Sam brings out from under his side of the bed.

"What…?" I take it from him. "For me?"

"Of course for you!" he laughs.

I pull the curling ribbon so that the beautiful bow loosens and gives way, enabling me to open the bag and pull out the tissue paper, which smells of citrus fruits and spices.

Beneath the paper is a small, neat wooden box. I pull it out of the bag, carefully opening it.

"What is it, Mummy? What did Father Christmas leave you?" Holly sounds almost jealous.

"I don't think this is really from Father Christmas." I slide a beautiful silver ring out of the box. It is a neat, solid band, with three little sapphires set inside. "Sam, it's beautiful."

He smiles at me. "Read the inscription. Inside."

I bring the ring close to my face and examine its curved interior.

For Alice, forever. S.

"Oh Sam," I say, my eyes filling with tears.

"It's an eternity ring," he says.

"What's a ternity ring?" asks Holly.

"It's an itternity ring," Ben corrects incorrectly. "It means forever, doesn't it, Mum?"

"It does," I say. I lean across to kiss Sam. "Thank you."

"I could only have up to twenty characters," he says, downplaying this beautiful gesture. That's why you got S and not Sam."

"Well I think I'll always know it stands for Sam. I love it."

I think of the set of books and the new jumper which await Sam downstairs. They don't stand up to this somehow. "We said we weren't going to spend much this year though!" I admonish.

"That's because I wanted to spend it on you. I wanted to get you this ring anyway, but today seemed like the right day for it. A little reminder that a husband's for life, not just for Christmas."

"Oh Sam. Thank you. Now I am definitely making the coffee."

I go downstairs, a spring in my step, well aware of the two pairs of little footsteps behind me. I stop. They stop too. And I turn suddenly, making Ben and Holly laugh. "What do you think you're up to?" I ask.

"We just want to look. Just a little look," says Ben, "under the tree."

"We won't touch anything," Holly says in her sweetest voice.

"Hmm… OK," I say. "But just wait a minute."

I go through the kitchen, wishing Meg a happy Christmas as I pass her bed. She opens her eyes and gives one cursory wag of her tail. I go into the lounge and switch on the Christmas tree lights. "OK," I call, standing back.

The other door opens and two little faces peer in and I wish I had a camera to capture their expressions. I know they do not need all these presents. I know that there are even more hidden away upstairs, and more still for Holly for her birthday. But nevertheless the pure delight and amazement on their faces as they gaze at the magical scene is something I would not want to have missed.

"Can we open one?" Ben tries his luck.

"No, not now. You know the rule." No under-the-tree presents till after breakfast.

"Can we have breakfast now?"

"Nice try, Holly! No, not yet. Go on, get back upstairs to Daddy and have a proper look at your stocking presents. I'll bring us all a drink."

"OK." They give in good-naturedly and I return to the kitchen. "Do you want to go out, Meg?" Her look says *Have you seen what time it is? Are you mad?*

"Fair enough," I laugh and busy myself making coffee and getting cups of squash and a couple of pre-packed chocolate croissants for Ben and Holly. That should help delay things just a little longer.

Back upstairs, we cosy up in bed and the strong coffee hits the spot so I don't feel quite as zombie-like as before. We listen to the Christmas songs on the radio and I read Holly the little book about a Christmas bear which she has had since she was a baby. I notice Ben is listening while pretending not to.

Eventually, they begin pleading again. I look at Sam. "I'll go and get breakfast on the go," he offers.

"And I'll have a quick shower," I say, "if you don't mind."

"Of course not. Kids, are you coming with me? You can watch some TV if you like but NO feeling the presents and trying to guess what they are, OK?"

"OK!" They look delightedly at each other.

"I mean it! says Sam.

Once they've trundled off downstairs, I pull out my clothes for the day and put my new ring on the bedside table along with my wedding ring. Then I pick the eternity ring up again and hold it to the light, turning it this way and that. It is perfect. Understated and beautiful.

I shower happily, singing to myself as I use the ginger-and-orange shower gel and shampoo I treated myself to. I step out of the heat of the shower cubicle, steam rising from my skin, and dry myself quickly, trying to maintain my body heat, then it's into the bedroom to get dressed and put my rings back on.

I remember the Christmastime when Sophie went missing, such a long time ago now. Once we knew that Sophie was safe, Sam and I had eventually swapped our gifts before the fire. I open my jewellery box now and find the pendant and chain he had given me. The stone on the pendant is garnet and I read again the little card that came with it:

Garnet is associated with romantic love and passion. It is thought to attract love and soul mates, to enhance self-esteem and encourage positive thinking.

Garnet is also known as a stone that can assist with success in one's career or business. It can be used to build self-confidence and to boost energy and creativity.

Soul mate, without a doubt, I think, and at that moment the opening notes of *Stay Another Day* by East 17 come on the radio and embarrassingly I find my eyes filling with tears, and a little lump rising up my throat. I am so grateful for Sam, for the children, but the thought of Sam's daughter has me thinking of all the people we're missing – as well as our lovely Sophie, my parents, Julie, Luke, Zinnia… even

Karen. I do love to see everybody at Christmas. It sometimes feels like the only time in the year when we can all stop and give each other our full attention. Still, this year I can give all of that to Sam and Ben and Holly. Without anybody else to think about, we can just cosy up and look after each other, and relax. That doesn't sound so bad.

By the time I'm dressed and back downstairs, my tears have dried up and I'm ready for breakfast. Sam has done scrambled eggs and toast, with hash browns and grilled tomatoes and beans. The plan is to go for a walk around lunchtime and have our Christmas dinner at teatime, so this breakfast needs to set us up for the day. I am quite sure there will be plenty of snacks in between though.

We sit and eat and it doesn't escape my notice that the children are gobbling down their breakfasts as fast as they possibly can. Sam, meanwhile, is taking his time.

"Mmmm," he says. "I've excelled myself here. And this hash brown is so delicious. Do you know what, I think I'm still hungry. I think I might have a second breakfast…"

"No, Daddy!" Holly is almost in tears. "You can't."

"We can't wait any longer," Ben says pleadingly.

"He's just teasing you," I say. "Come on, let's get our things in the dishwasher and then…"

"Open presents?" suggests Holly.

"Yes!" I laugh. "Open presents."

The children are unusually helpful when it comes to clearing the table. I am pleased to see that Meg has eaten all of her scrambled eggs and toast. While she has an appetite I think all must be OK. I push away the thought that next year might be the one where we lose her. But she might surprise us yet.

I go through to the lounge and see Ben and Holly on the

floor by the tree, poised as if waiting for the starter pistol.

"OK, how are we going to do this?" asks Sam. "Alice, do you want to pass the presents around? You know what's what with the wrapping paper."

"I think I do," I say, doubting myself. "Now, let's see, this one is for Ben, and this one is for Holly... these are from us."

I pass across two of the more boring presents. Pyjamas for both. They rip off the wrapping paper and put the presents aside, eyes returning immediately to the pile of gifts.

"These," I say, "are from Granny Karen and Ron..." I hope I have remembered the paper correctly but it's not too hard as Karen is quite a traditionalist when it comes to gender so Holly's paper is all kittens and butterflies, while Ben's has puppies playing with balls. To be fair, it does make my job easier.

"Oh my god!" Ben shouts, brandishing a much-sought-after robot toy that he has been dropping heavy-handed hints about for months.

"Language, Ben!" I say.

"What?" he looks annoyed. "I wasn't swearing."

"Well, yes, but..." I look at Sam, floundering. I was brought up not to say things like *oh my god*, but I am not one hundred percent sure why.

Sam just shrugs. "Some people would be offended by it, Benny," he says. "What have you got, Holly?"

Holly is already clutching to her chest a beautiful baby doll toy. I groan inwardly at the clear gender lines Karen is drawing but Holly clearly immediately loves her doll, and Ben his robot, so I have nowhere to go with this really.

"Here," Sam says, aware of how I feel about these things.

"These are from me and Mummy." He picks up two matching boxes. "You need to open them at the same time, OK?"

"OK," they shout.

"Three… two… one…" Sam says. Ben and Holly rip into the wrapping paper and reveal a remote-control car each.

"Yes!" Ben punches the air.

"Yes!" Holly copies him.

"We can charge them up and take them out in the street later," says Sam.

Then I hand Sam a gift from me, though it pales in comparison to the beautiful ring which I just can't stop looking at. He opens the box. "Kate Atkinson books!" he grins. "You shouldn't have!"

"You will love them, I know it." I have been trying to convince him to read the *Case Histories* books for ages; he is more of a non-fiction kind of reader but I really want Sam to get into some novels. Now it just seems a bit mean, given his beautiful, generous gift to me.

He laughs though. "Haven't you already got these yourself?"

"Yes, but mine are dog-eared, and a bit wrinkly. Like me. Whereas these," I say, taking the first of the books and stroking it, "are shiny and beautiful, like you."

"Hmm," he laughs again. "Keep talking."

But the children have no time for this and instead are already edging towards the mounds of presents, eager for more.

"Hang on," says Sam. "Before you open any more, let's get these cars out of the boxes as they might take a while to charge."

It's a relief, even after just these few presents, to take a breather, but it's not long before they are back and it soon becomes a bit of a free-for-all.

"Don't forget once they're open, that's it," I say, but my words fall on deaf ears and I can't really say I blame them. Put a huge pile of colourful gifts in front of a six-year-old and eight-year-old and what do you expect? However, as the number of unwrapped presents rapidly overtakes the number still under the tree, I'm glad we kept aside those from Mum and Dad, and Holly's birthday gifts. Though I feel like it's a bit of a shame that Christmas is overriding her birthday, she doesn't seem too perturbed right now. The tears are almost guaranteed to come later: that classic combination of over-excitement and early start, and the gradual anti-climax once there are no presents left to open. I am already prepared for both children to lose it at some point.

With perfect timing, however, my phone goes just as the children have a small pile of gifts left, and I know it's just books and chocolate. I pick up my phone. "It's Mum and Dad!" I say and answer to see my parents' smiling faces filling my screen.

"Happy Christmas!" they call.

I hold the phone so they can see us all. "Happy Christmas! Kids, are you going to say hello to Granny and Grandad?"

"Happy Christmas!" Ben shouts and Holly, as ever, follows suit.

"Happy Christmas Phil and Sue!" Sam calls.

"How are you all? Did Father Christmas come?" Mum asks.

I manoeuvre the phone to give a sweeping view of the piles of toys and screwed-up wrapping paper. "As you can see, yes." I sent Mum a message late last night so she knows that the children won't have had their gifts from her and Dad yet.

"Wow!" Dad's eyes grow wide at the sight. I know he'll be thinking of his own childhood Christmases, and how things have changed. Many's the time I've heard his tales of the few gifts they'd have had and how they loved them all the more for it. I know he is right but this is how life is right now. I don't know how to do things differently, but I do feel a slight unease deep within about just how much our children have and how this leads them to expect more of the same. But they're good kids. Lovely kids. I know I'm biased, but they are.

"How's your day been so far?" I ask.

"Hot!" laughs Mum.

"Not very Christmassy," admits Dad. "I've been for a swim up on the top deck."

"Just as long as it's not overboard," says Sam. "That sounds nice though!"

"It is," Dad doesn't sound quite convinced, "but we miss you all. Your mum and I were saying, weren't we Sue, I don't think we'll go away for Christmas again."

"But Alice and Sam might not want us at theirs every year!" Mum says.

"They can come to us," says Dad.

"That's not really what I meant." Mum smiles.

We tell her and Dad about the day so far, and Ben and Holly show them some of their toys. I am pleased they're both excited to talk about their cars and they take the phone from me so that they can show them to Mum and Dad. I hear my parents making the correct impressed noises.

And then it's time for them to go – already lunchtime where they are.

"Bye loves," Mum says, and I see she looks a bit sad. "We miss you all so much."

"We miss you too Mum," I say. "Happy Christmas."

They both wave and their image remains frozen on the screen for a moment, and then they are gone, and the rooms feels a little bit emptier.

Sam puts his hand on my shoulder. "Come on, let's have another coffee, shall we?"

"Sounds great," I say.

"And kids, how about watching some Christmas TV? *The Snowman and the Snowdog*?"

"Alright Dad," Ben says. He and Holly both look a little bit tired, and pale. I check Holly's blood glucose is OK and see she's edging towards being a bit low.

"Would you like a snack as well? Some chocolate biscuits?"

"Yes please!"

So they settle on the sofa together and I get them each a little plate with some biscuits and a glass of milk. While Holly nibbles a biscuit, I fiddle about with her pump, trying to make sure she gets enough insulin to deal with the biscuits but not so much that it's going to send her levels lower. It's a delicate balance to strike and I by no means always get it right.

I'm just tucking the pump back into the little pouch she wears around her waist when the doorbell goes.

"Who's that going to be?" I ask myself more than the children. "It's Christmas Day."

Ben and Holly's eyes have pretty much glazed over as they watch the TV and they barely register that there is somebody at the door. I hear Sam open it, and low voices, and then he calls me.

I straighten up and go through to the hallway to see that it's Natalie, and she's in tears.

19

"He cancelled our gas," she sobs as I usher her in and Sam makes himself scarce, going through to the lounge. "And the electricity."

"What? How? Why?"

"I don't know. He came in the other day, when he brought Bobby and Courtney back from the zoo. I think he did it then."

"Where are the kids now?" I ask.

"At home, they're watching something on my phone," she says. "I- I'm sorry to disturb you on Christmas but I didn't know who else I could go to. I just want some hot water please if that's OK." She presents me with a flask.

"Oh Natalie," I hug her. "Of course it's OK. I can't believe this."

"I know. And he redirected their presents too – had them sent up to his mum's in Gloucester. They were all meant to arrive yesterday but only the trampoline turned up here and it's in a heap in the garage. I started putting it together last night after they'd gone to bed but Courtney woke up and started crying and I had to go and see her, and it was so cold in the garage later, and I only had the light from my phone because the electricity had gone off. I thought it was a power cut at first but then I could see all the other lights were on in the street. Anyway, if I put it up in the garage, how could I have got it into the garden, I wasn't thinking straight…"

I can feel her nerves and her bewilderment, and panic. I can feel utter hatred rising up in me for this man who is meant to be a husband and father.

"It's unbelievable," I storm quietly, not wanting to alert my children but thinking of all the toys and books and clothes and sweets lying piled up in our lounge, and imagining poor Natalie's children waking up to nothing.

"How are Bobby and Courtney?" I ask quietly.

"Oh my god, they were inconsolable this morning… I had to make something up. I can't remember what I said, something about there being a power cut and affecting Santa, or some rubbish, I don't know, I… I don't suppose it made any sense to them."

Natalie is shaking and I can feel myself tense up with utter disgust and anger and indignation. Women and children suffer at hands of men like Rob all the time. It's overlooked, brushed aside, swept right under the carpet. Maybe Rob has never hit Natalie. Maybe he never will. But he has taken over her life, made her beholden to him, and now he's using that power to punish her for standing up to him – and he's using the children to do it. He must know how heartbroken they will be, and he'll also know it is Natalie who has to bear the brunt of it. *Please, please, don't ever take him back*, I think as I begin to fill Natalie's flask with hot water. Then I look round our ridiculously overstocked kitchen and wonder what I'm doing. I put the lid on her flask then I dig out a couple of ours. I take the coffee that

Sam has just made and fill one flask with it, then I make up some hot chocolate in the other, and pull biscuits out from the cupboard, some bags of crisps, a jar of olives and a box of dates. "I'm making you a hamper," I say.

"Oh Alice, you don't need to do that."

"It's nothing," I say, rooting around for some nice snacks which take little preparation. "Honestly. Look, I've got some noodles here, which you can make up with hot water, and you can have these crackers... and this houmous, and these breadsticks..." I start to fill a picnic bag for her. I put in a mini bottle of prosecco although that seems almost like rubbing it in. I don't suppose Natalie feels like celebrating. "I did pop round to see you last night, but your house was in darkness so I thought you'd managed to get up to your mum's. Now I realise why your lights were off. Are you sure Rob did this?" I am still struggling to believe that even he could be such a bastard.

"Yes," she nods. "He told me himself. He's up at his mum's now too. I spoke to her and she's as bad as he is. Says it's what I should expect for kicking him out. They're coming down later today to pick up the children."

"But they can't!" I exclaim. "You can't let them!"

"It's better for the kids, isn't it, to go somewhere warm where they'll have nice beds and hot food and they can have their presents then too. They'll know Santa hasn't forgotten them. It's better for them." She sounds like she is trying to convince herself.

"Well yes in a way, but they won't have you. This is really not fair."

"I know. But what can I do? He's their dad and he's got everything, and I've got nothing. Anyway thank you Alice, it's so kind of you. I don't want to ruin your day."

"Honestly you're not, and it's nothing," I say again, handing over the hamper. "I hope this helps a bit."

"It really does." She offers a sad smile. "You're a good friend. Thank you. I'd better get back now.'

"If there's anything I can do…" I offer lamely and the words resound with me more than they ever have before. I stand at the door and watch Natalie walk along the street, towards the illuminated reindeer and past all the homes that are filled with happy families. Jill and Raymond will have their son and his wife and their children round. I picture the difference between the two mirror-image next-door houses, with light and warmth and laughter in one and two children huddled round their mum's phone in the other, sitting in relative darkness on this dull, grey day.

I go back into our house, where both children are snuggled up to Sam, Meg on the floor just in front of them.

"Everything alright?" Sam asks.

"Yeah, of course," I smile brightly. "I just need to make some more coffee. Could you give me a hand please?"

He takes the hint and extricates himself from the children, following me into the kitchen.

"What the fuck!" he says as I tell him what's happened.

"I know. So I packed up some of our stuff for them, but it… it's not right, is it?"

"No," says Sam grimly. "It's not."

"I mean… not just what Rob's done, but letting them sit in that house in the cold."

"No," Sam says, catching my meaning.

"So would you mind if I…?"

"Of course not!" he says. "It's Christmas, isn't it? And even if it wasn't…"

I run out into the street, down the road to Natalie's. Despite my disgust and anger at Rob I suddenly feel brighter, to be doing this. To be able to actually help, if Natalie will let me. I knock on her door.

Nothing. Of course, she'll be scared it might be Rob. I lift her letterbox open.

"Natalie," I call as softly as I can. "It's just me, Alice."

"It's Alice, Mummy," I hear Bobby's voice, and then there are footsteps.

"Alice," Natalie says, unable to stop herself from peering down the street.

"It really is just me," I say, and I see the bag I gave her is just inside the door. "I'm taking that back, if you don't mind." She looks surprised, but resigned. Life is like this. You are given something good, it gets taken away. I don't want her thinking that and I quickly elaborate. "We want you to come to us. You and Bobby and Courtney. Come and have Christmas at our house. Please. We'd love to have you. If you'd like to, that is."

Natalie's lip quivers. "Really?"

"Really," I say. "Of course. I should have offered straightaway, I'm sorry."

"Oh Alice, thank you. Thank you so much."

"It's nothing," I say and this time those words don't feel so empty. "Honestly, we're used to having lots of people around us at Christmas and we'd be so happy for you three to join us."

Bobby and Courtney are standing in the lounge doorway. I notice they are wearing their coats, and their hats. It's not a very cold day but in a house with no heating they will feel it. My heart breaks for them that they went through Christmas Eve in the dark, and that they woke up to no presents. Rob must have a heart of stone, if indeed he has a heart at all.

"Would you like to go to Ben and Holly's?" Natalie asks them and their faces light up.

"On Christmas?" asks Courtney.

"Yes!" I say. "On Christmas! Come and celebrate with us. We would absolutely love to have you."

20

Even as we walk down the road, Courtney holding my hand and skipping, I see thin, watery sunshine seeping through the cloud cover. I can feel how tense Natalie is, and I know she must be on the look-out for Rob and his mum. I must admit I'm not 100% relaxed about this myself – I could do without a confrontation at our house or another black eye for Sam when the first one's only just healing – but there is no way I'm going to leave Natalie and her children to deal with this on their own. There is strength and safety in numbers. I just wish that Julie was here too. She is more formidable than me. I will just have to channel her spirit if it comes to it.

Ben and Holly are delighted to see their friends as the festive shine has begun to dim somewhat now that to their minds all the presents have been opened. Tiredness is creeping in and the magic of the day has begun to ebb away. It is a long day, to be honest, and I find I'm genuinely glad to have some extra people around. As Sam, Natalie and I go into the kitchen, the children head up to Ben's room. I'm glad that Sam had the foresight to help them tidy up their piles of Christmas gifts so that the lounge is not strewn with reminders of what Courtney and Bobby are missing.

"All they've got is that trampoline," Natalie says, "and I couldn't even manage to put that together for them."

"Do you want me to take a look?" Sam asks.

"Oh no, you don't need to…"

"I'd love to," he says.

"It's true," I tell her. "He loves building things. Think of it as a Christmas present for him."

Natalie laughs and takes a tissue to blow her nose. "Alright then. If you're sure."

"I don't need telling twice," says Sam. Natalie hands him her keys and explains how to get into the garage. He wastes no time in heading over. *Be careful*, I want to say to him, trying not to think of what Rob will do if he returns to his house to find Sam in the garage making his children's trampoline. But I don't want to make Natalie feel worse.

"Coffee?" I ask her. "Or tea? Or you're welcome to have something stronger…"

"Oh no, tea will be just fine, thank you."

"Herbal or normal?"

"If you've got herbal that would be perfect."

"Good idea." I don't think I can take any more caffeine right now; it will only make me edgy and even more tired.

I pull out my box of potions and Natalie laughs. "That's quite the selection!"

"Ah yes, well it's really all down to my friend Lizzie, who used to run the yoga classes and retreats at Amethi. She was very keen on her teas and it's rubbed off on me."

"She sounds brilliant. Does she still work there?"

"No, it's really all changed there now. And actually Lizzie is off galivanting round Europe in a van, with her partner."

166

"That sounds tempting," says Natalie wistfully.

"It does, doesn't it? Except –" I break off and smile at the sound of a peal of laughter from upstairs – "it could get a bit crowded with certain little people bouncing off the walls."

"Yeah. And I can't say I fancy being stuck in a confined space with Rob," Natalie admits.

"No. I don't suppose you do." I make a pot of Christmas blend tea and we take it through to the lounge, Meg at our heels. As I pour our drinks, the aroma of mixed spices fills the air and sunshine begins to stream through the windows so that it feels almost springlike. With a friend round and the children playing upstairs, it's like any other play date and I have to remind myself it's actually Christmas Day.

I notice Natalie is sitting hunched forwards, clutching her cup. I gently take it from her and place it on a table. "Sit back," I say. "Relax. You are allowed to, you know."

There is something in her posture that I recognise; it takes me back to my time with Geoff. I often had neck ache then, or pains in my back, and it took me a long time to realise it was because I was always on edge. Even sitting down at home, watching TV, I wouldn't allow myself to relax. I forgot that I was able to, and that I was allowed to enjoy my life. I just wanted to keep things steady and stable and make sure Geoff was appeased. My natural tendency is to avoid confrontation and unpleasantness wherever possible; I suppose Geoff recognised that and used it as leverage to get his own way.

Natalie looks at me. "How did it come to this, Alice?"

"I don't know," I say, finding my own tears springing out in sympathy. "But I do know it's not because of anything you did. Just in case you're thinking of blaming yourself."

I in fact think that I do know, or have some idea. Just as Geoff took advantage of me when I was at a low ebb, Rob has done the same with Natalie. She was a vulnerable young mum living with her own mother, probably sleep-deprived and hurting from the break-up with Bobby's dad. Along came Rob; a knight in shining armour, as I am sure he would have painted himself. Lifting her out of the monotony of new motherhood and telling her all the things she wanted to hear. Once he'd won her over, prised her away from the life she knew, like shucking an oyster, he would have had her right where he wanted her. With no job, no car and no driving licence anyway, not to mention a young child to look after, Natalie was dependent on Rob and really at his mercy. Becoming pregnant with Courtney just served to seal the deal.

None of this feels very Christmassy though, and I am not sure Natalie would want to be reminded of it anyway. I am certain she knows where and how things went wrong. All we can do now is look at how to put them right again. But first and foremost, it is Christmas, and we have four little children for whom we need to keep the magic alive.

***

After an hour or so, Sam comes back. His clothes are dirty and one of his hands is bleeding a bit but he's grinning.

"Did you win?" I ask.

"I'm pleased to say I did. One trampoline ready and waiting in your garden." He bows to Natalie, who smiles.

"Oh my god, thank you so much. Honestly. Thank you, both of you. I can't thank you enough. I'm so sorry for ruining your Christmas."

"You've got to stop saying that!" I smile. "You have not ruined our Christmas. Now, when do you want to do the great trampoline reveal?"

There is a lot of banging and thumping from upstairs.

Sam looks at us. "Elephants?"

"It would seem that way," Natalie says. "How about we go now? If you don't mind. I mean, you don't have to come. I can just take Bobby and Courtney, you probably have family things to do…"

"We'd love to come," I say. "And I'm afraid you're stuck with us for today, unless you've had enough of us already."

"I don't think so! But really, honestly, if you'd rather just get back to your family Christmas…"

"Natalie!" I say. "I am banning you from saying anything along those lines again. This is *our* Christmas now."

"Alright," she smiles. "Then let's go. I might have to say Father Christmas made a late delivery."

"I think that's a great idea," says Sam.

We go to the bottom of the stairs and call the children down. It takes a while for everyone to get their shoes and coats on, but once we're ready we make a very merry little band walking along to Natalie's house. Jill and Raymond wave out of their front window and Raymond mouths something.

"What's he saying?" Sam asks. "Probably swearing at us knowing Potty Mouth Raymond."

That makes Natalie chuckle, knowing how straight-laced her neighbours are. "He told Bobby he and Jill and the family would be going to church this morning and Bobby was outraged – 'But it's Christmas!' he said, like 'why would you want to ruin Christmas by going to church?' – I don't think Raymond was very amused."

We go into the garden via the side gate, Natalie leading the way. She stops at the end of the path and turns to Sam, mouthing 'Thank you'. "Bobby, Courtney, come here. I knew Father Christmas wouldn't have forgotten you!"

They run forward and both gasp, Courtney jumping up and down and clapping her hands. I follow on and see that my amazing husband has not only finished putting up the trampoline but he's taken the huge bow from the hamper from Lydia and Si, and fixed it to the zip-up door on the outer netting. He has also, I see, wound solar lights around the very top of the netting, but we won't see the benefit of them until later.

I take his hand as Natalie's children run across the garden, closely followed by our two.

"I love you," I smile at Sam. He kisses me, just as Natalie turns to look at us. I feel bad, that she sees this when she must be feeling so awful about her own relationship, but she smiles at us.

"They love it!" she says, as the children kick off their shoes and clamber up the little ladder.

"Careful!" says Sam. "Just watch out for each other. We don't want any trips to A&E. You'll see all sorts there on Christmas Day."

"Oh, and merry Christmas kids," I say, laughing.

"That too!" he smiles.

It is lovely seeing the four children playing together like this, and I'm very happy to just sit in Natalie's garden while we watch them. I've told Sam about Rob's threat to come and collect Bobby and Courtney and I know we three adults are keeping an ear out. Natalie is a bit jumpy at the sound of any car engines or doors slamming, so after a while I ask if she'd rather come back to ours now.

"Ohhhhh," chorus the kids in disappointment.

"Don't worry, the trampoline isn't going anywhere!" I say. "And maybe we can have a snack and then we could go down to the beach for a bit?" I look at Natalie.

She smiles and nods. "That sounds lovely. As long as you're sure you don't mind…"

I give her a look. "Alright, alright!" she laughs. "I promise to stop now."

On the way back to our house, my phone beeps. It's the alarm telling me Holly's blood sugars are going low. It's not surprising, given all the excitement and the jumping around she's been doing.

"Holly, have a couple of these," I say, handing her some jelly babies as soon as we step inside the front door.

Natalie looks at me. "Is Holly diabetic?"

"Yes," I say, surprised she didn't already know this. It just shows how successful I've been in my keeping her at arm's length. I think I've stepped back from telling people recently, scared of their reaction and them saying something stupid to Holly.

"My little brother's diabetic," she says. "Since he was four."

"No way," I say, trying not to sound too delighted. I of course do not wish for anybody to have diabetes, but it's always such a relief to meet somebody who actually understands. Then, cautiously, I ask, "How's he doing?"

"Tom? He's absolutely brilliant. He's got the sensor like Holly has and I know it's made life a lot easier for him because he does a lot of sport and loves going to the gym and all that. It's hard work though, isn't it?"

"Yes," I say. "It is." I walk through to the kitchen and Natalie follows me.

"I didn't really get it, growing up," she says. "It was more annoying than anything but Mum's told me about it since I've had Bobby and Courtney, so I know what to look out for, and I've realised how hard it was for her bringing us up. My dad died when I was eight so it was just the three of us."

Bloody hell, I'm learning a lot about Natalie. I feel suddenly incredibly fond of her, and full of admiration too. She must be a few years younger than me and it brings out a sisterly, almost maternal, feeling, but I don't think she'd want that. She and I have children the same age. We are both adults. We are equals.

"You've definitely been through it, Natalie." She is still going through it, I remind myself.

"Well, yeah, I guess. There's always somebody worse off though, isn't there? I know it's a cliché but it's true."

"I've got some non-alcoholic wine here," I say, rooting through the fridge. "Would you like a glass? We can have a proper drink later if you like."

"Go on then," she smiles and I feel like I am beginning to see the real Natalie. The one that isn't a bag of nerves and self-doubt.

"Sam," I call, "come and drink a toast with us."

He comes into the kitchen and I hand him a glass, and we all raise our glasses, clinking them together and then taking a sip. It's very nice. Maybe being teetotal wouldn't be too bad.

"Is it wrong to say happy Christmas?" Sam asks, looking from me to Natalie. I look at her too.

"No, of course not. It is a happy Christmas," she says and she raises her glass again. "To both of you. Thank you."

21

We have some of the crackers and cheese from the hamper for lunch and then Natalie and I get ready for the beach. Ben and Bobby want to stay and play with the remote-control cars and Sam is happy to do the same.

"No gender stereotyping here," I smile at Natalie.

We go to her house to collect Courtney's waterproofs and wellies. I don't want Natalie going anywhere on her own today. We come back home, get the girls (including Meg) ready, and then pile into the car.

The day has really bloomed and there are moments of almost warmth at the beach, when the sun breaks free and soaks us all with its very welcome light. The two girls dig holes and look for sand worms and little creatures in the shallows and the rock pools, while Natalie and I sit on a blanket, snug in thick coats, woolly hats and gloves. Meg sits contentedly by my side, looking out across the waves, her grey muzzle lifted to appreciate the smells of the sea. Out on the rocks, a pair of cormorants stand, spreading their wings, stock-still like a pair of martial arts masters.

"This is really nice, Alice. Thank you."

"It's a pleasure. And what a day it's turning out to be!" I

can feel the sunshine on my face and I close my eyes briefly. "I half wish I'd brought my swimming stuff down here."

"Would you go in today? Really?"

"Yes! Maybe not for long but a dip. It settles me somehow, levels everything out. And nobody else in the family wants to do it so I get a few moments to myself."

She smiles. "Could I come sometime, give it a go? If I promise not to talk too much." She grins suddenly.

"Of course. But only if we swim in absolute silence."

We both laugh. It feels good, having her company. We are side by side, coat sleeves touching, and I realise I feel relaxed with her. I would not have expected to, a couple of weeks back. I've been running away from her and it's not very nice of me. I think what I tell the children: *Be kind to everyone. You don't have to be best friends but give everybody a chance. Don't let anyone feel left out.*

I don't think I've been leading by example with Natalie and, knowing what I know now, I am ashamed of myself. Still, I cannot go back. The only way to make things better is in what I do from now on.

"Will you stay here, do you think?" I ask.

"In Cornwall?"

"No, on the beach." I nudge her and she laughs but then she's serious again.

"I've been thinking about this. I'm only here because of Rob and his job. I don't have any friends here, not really. And Mum is so far away, and I miss her and Tom – my brother. But the children are getting settled and making friends, and it is such a lovely place."

I had held back when she said she didn't have friends here. Sitting here with her now, I realise I would like to get to know her better, be a friend to her. I'd like her to be my friend. Although, will she want that? Today is a day of crisis, but it won't be like this every day. I think about how she has been a bit distant with me recently. I can't really blame her.

"It is lovely," I say. "And it does take a while to settle in somewhere new. It took me and Julie a long time to really feel like it was home."

"Really?"

"Of course!" I find myself telling her our story – how we first came here as fresh-faced eighteen-year-olds and then came back ten years later. How Julie had been a bit of a nightmare, but I had been a bit judgemental, and we'd almost fallen out. I tell her about seeing Sam again and meeting Kate and not realising the two of them had been together. And how Sophie is not Sam's daughter biologically but she is in every way that matters.

Natalie takes it all in, listening intently. "Bloody hell Alice, I just assumed you and Sam had been together forever. And the way you talk about Julie, I'd never imagined you falling out with each other."

"No, I don't suppose I've told you all that much really. I do tend to keep things to myself these days. It's being in a small town. You have to really know you can trust someone." I think of Belinda Carmichael and how she seems to love nothing better than to share other people's news. Maybe there is more to her than meets the eye, if I'm being generous, but I don't think I'll be going to any great lengths to find out.

Courtney and Holly come running up the beach.

"Happy Christmas, Alice," Courtney says, handing me a stone which is still wet and shining. A streak of orangey-red runs through its centre. "It's pretty, like you."

175

"Oh Courtney," I say. "Thank you so much. I love it." She beams at me. I realise that the night is coming up fast now and the girls' faces and hands look red and cold. "Shall we go back home? There's Christmas dinner to eat yet."

I see a slight reluctance on Natalie's face as we stand up, shaking the sand off us. *Back to reality*, I think. Except it's not. It's back to our house. It's back to Christmas.

"Come on!" I say, clipping Meg's lead on her and casting one last glance out towards the sea before heading back to the car. "We'll have a proper drink back at the house. And Sam messaged to say the boys are playing inside now and he's starting to get the food ready."

"He's a lovely man."

"He is. But I have to tell you, it's not going to be your average Christmas dinner. There's no turkey because we don't eat meat. Well Sam does sometimes, but not today. He's got some salmon, and Ben's trying that too. Holly is having fish fingers. I'm having mushroom wellington. Then there's mashed potato, roast potatoes, roast veg, gravy, Yorkshire puds, even some chips… basically, we are all going to have what we like. There is loads of it all, and I'm not saying that to show off but to say that you three can choose whatever you want."

"Can I give you some money for it?"

"No, you really don't have to do that. Honestly, Natalie, we've been spoiled this year. Every year, probably. But I've had gifts from people Julie and I used to work with; gifts from people I work with now, and then this blooming massive hamper yesterday from some old friends. It's far too much for the four of us. It makes me guilty thinking about it to be honest, you'll be doing me a favour if you share it with us. And I think our parents have probably been trying to compensate for not being here so they've overdone it on the present front…"

I have an idea suddenly, and while Natalie clips the girls into their car seats and I settle Meg in the boot, I send Sam a message. I wait for his reply. It makes me smile.

Getting into the car I say, "Let's have a drive round town, look at all the Christmas decorations, shall we?"

"Why not?" Natalie says contentedly and I sneak a look at her, noticing she looks relatively relaxed and definitely better for having some fresh air and time by the sea.

I switch the engine on and take my time tracing the outline of the town, all the way to the top so that we are nearly home but then I sweep back round and down again, past Mum and Dad's house and towards the harbour. We admire different Christmas trees and house decorations along the way, marking them out of ten and choosing our favourites. Then we trace the road along the harbourside, seeing the lifeboat station decked out in Christmas finery and all the restaurants, bars and shops following suit. I take the sharp left up Fore Street and drive along the narrow, cobbled road, which is for once devoid of shoppers and almost eerily peaceful. A ginger cat takes a break from licking its back leg to watch us as we pass by, following the strings of warm yellow lights which create a canopy along the length of the street and guide us towards the large star which shines down on the town from the church spire.

At the end we take the sharp turn which has us heading up towards the Bay Hotel. It looks very imposing, almost haughty, looking down on its neighbouring B&Bs. It is very grand, though, bedecked in ruby-red lights.

"Just one more stop!" I say. "The Island." I may be playing for time but I really would like to pay a little visit to the Island – my favourite place within my favourite town – and pay my respects on this special day. We have to retrace our journey along the harbour front and I can sense the girls getting a bit restless in the back but I also think Natalie is enjoying the journey, knowing she is safe and contained in this warm space and there is no way that Rob can intrude on this bit of time.

The Island car park is half empty and I easily find a space next to the grass.

"Shall we go up to the chapel?" I ask.

The girls are fairly sure they don't want to.

"You go up Alice, I'll stay here," Natalie says.

"Are you sure?" I feel a bit rude just running off but I really would like to go up there. Pay my respects, if that doesn't sound too weird.

"Absolutely!" she smiles.

"I won't be long."

I waste no time getting out of the car and striding across the grass. Time was when I'd have had Meg with me but it feels kinder to let her rest now. I follow the 'scramble' route we took the other day, ignoring the concrete pavement in favour of the lesser trodden path up through the shrubbery and over the little rocky outcrop. I know I'm getting muddy but I don't care. There! I emerge from the shrubbery to the surprise of an older couple who are standing on the steps to the chapel, looking back towards the town. I grin at them. "Happy Christmas!" I call, knowing full well I must look a bit mad.

"Happy Christmas," they say, smiling.

"We should take that route back down," says the man.

"We will not!" his partner whacks him on the arm and they both laugh.

I pass them by and go up to the chapel itself, laying my hand against the cool stone wall. This is as close to a religious experience as I have, coming here. I walk around to the other side, where Sam and I stood with Ben and Holly just yesterday, and from where I can look across the waves. There are white tops out there and I see rain clouds far out across the sea, casting dark shadows over the water. We'll be home before they reach us.

I breathe in slowly, and out even slower, and I smile. A gull swoops low, at eye level for me, momentarily almost still as the different air flows converge, then it swoops and glides downwards, descending onto one of the grassy rocks further towards the sea.

I know I shouldn't be too long. I walk back to the other side of the chapel and note that the couple are a way down the path now. I am quite alone.

I look at the town, windows glinting in the winter sunlight, and just think *Thank you*. I don't know who I'm thanking or whether it is just the town itself, but I know I am grateful, and so lucky.

I head back down the hill, the way I came, and I wave at the car, although I can't see inside to know whether they are looking at me. I accelerate, laughing for the sheer joy of the open space and this sense of freedom.

"Hi!" I say breathlessly as I open the door. And to Natalie, "Thanks for that."

"No problem. I've never been up there."

"What? Well, we'll have to rectify that. When we come for a swim."

She smiles and I start the engine. It's only as I'm swinging the car round that I see it. In the very far corner of the car park, a motor home.

179

"No…" I say.

"What?" Natalie asks.

"Over there. It looks like my parents' friend's van. But he's meant to be in Devon."

"Oh really?"

"Yes," I say thoughtfully as I drive slowly around the car park towards the mobile home. The lights are on inside it.

"I'm going to knock," I decide suddenly.

"What if it's not him?"

"I'll just apologise and we'll move on. Sorry girls, won't be a moment, then we'll head home, I promise."

I pull up a few spaces away and get out of the car. I look at the mobile home and wonder what I'm doing. It could be anyone in there. I try to listen in case there's a clue but although the lights are on all is quiet.

What am I doing? I shake my head and go back to the car.

"It can't be him," I say to Natalie. "I'm sure Mum and Dad said he's in Devon with his niece. I don't want to disturb whoever's in there. Let's just get home, shall we?"

"Yeahhh!" shouts Holly and Courtney copies her. It's funny seeing Holly as the older one for a change.

As we sweep back round the car park towards the exit I look up towards the chapel. The sky behind it is still blue but the sun seems to be sinking fast now, sitting lower in the sky and suggesting that Christmas Day – this one solitary day which has been built up to for months, which the children have been talking about practically since they returned to school in September, and which has taken over shop shelves, TV screens, radio channels and social media for weeks – is beginning to draw to a close.

No, I think. *That's where you're wrong.* Because I happen to know there is still a lot more of Christmas to enjoy.

22

When we get home I say to Natalie to hang on for a second. "I just need to go and check something." I open the front door and call "Hello?" quietly.

Sam pops his head out of the lounge door.

"Did you manage it?" I ask.

"Yes, the boys have been up in Ben's room for ages. They went quiet for a while and I was a bit worried but I went to check on them and they were just intently building a Lego theme park."

The image makes me smile. "And did you speak to Mum and Dad?"

"Yep, they thought it was a lovely idea and were more than happy to help. I said you'd give them a ring later."

"Thank you." I kiss him. "I'd better get them in now, can't leave them in the car forever! Do you want to call the boys down?"

Sam pulls the lounge door shut and goes upstairs to fetch the boys, while I go out and get Meg from the boot, telling Natalie and the girls they can go into the house but they have to wait in the hallway.

We gather in the small space and then Sam opens the

door to the lounge. The girls gasp. The curtains are closed and the room is illuminated by the lights on the tree and a whole array of battery-powered tealights he has put on every available surface. There is soft music playing and he must be using the oil burner too as there is a distinct scent of ginger and cloves on the air. The pièce de résistance can be found under the tree itself where the empty space left after the manic flurry of present-opening earlier has been filled anew with beautifully wrapped parcels and gift bags. The children gasp and run towards them.

"This one's got Courtney's name on!" says Ben, turning to the little girl. He is nice with her, accustomed as he is to having a little sister. "And this one's mine, and this is yours, Bobby…"

"Alright, hang on!" I laugh. "Just take a moment. Isn't this amazing!"

Natalie, meanwhile, is quiet. I look at her. She returns my look and I see her eyes are glistening. "What…?"

I put my hand on her arm and speak quietly. "I'll explain later. Just – well, I hope you're OK with this. But I wanted it to be a surprise for you as much as the children."

"It's too much," she says, and I wonder if I've really misread the situation. I've stepped in with my big feet and tried to save the day but it's not really my place to do that, is it? But – "I mean, it's overwhelming. It's – it's so lovely. Thank you, Alice. And you too, Sam."

He smiles. "Really, it's our pleasure. This is a lovely Christmas – I feel like if it was just us, we'd have been conked out on the settee by now. Anyway… I don't think we can hold this lot back any longer! Come on kids, let's see what we've got here, shall we?"

And Sam sits himself on the floor by the tree, surrounded

by children who look to him eagerly as he pulls out presents and hands them to the appropriate child. He already knows what is what because while we were out, driving around town, he's been on a call to Mum and Dad, asking if they'd mind if we do this and then working out what each parcel and bag contains and which child it might best be addressed to. I knew my parents would be up for this if Sam could explain what's been going on. I'm so pleased and so proud of them all.

Natalie and I sit on the floor too and help the children unwrap their gifts. There are books and clothes and toys and chocolate. I know Mum has been picking things up all over the place and some of these will be pre-loved (not the chocolate, I hope) but it doesn't make any difference to the children. I am grateful too that they don't ask where the presents have come from – and does it really matter? I look at the heaps of things my children have received today. And we still have presents to come from Sophie when she comes down later this week, not to mention Holly's birthday presents tucked away too.

I hope we can get away with leaving them until the day after Boxing Day, when she has her party with her friends. I feel like she's almost forgotten herself that it's her birthday, and I suppose it is a different experience. This day does not feel like it is about her in the same way that Ben's is about him. We'll just have to make sure that her party day is extra special. I may be biased but she deserves to be celebrated.

"Here, Natalie. This is for you," says Sam, handing her a bag. I look at him, wondering what it is. I had felt bad that there was nothing for Natalie. She looks at me. I smile, not sure whether to let on that I have no idea what it is.

She opens the bag and pulls out the set of Kate Atkinson books I'd given Sam.

"Oh, this is great!" Natalie says. "I've really got out of the habit of reading. Maybe this will get me back into it."

"I hope you'll like them as much as I do," I smile and sneak a look at Sam over the top of her head. He grins cheekily.

"I'm sure I will," Natalie says. "Thank you. But I haven't got anything for you…"

"Don't even think about it!" I say. "Honestly, Natalie, we've been beyond spoiled, all of us. And like Sam says, it's been so good having you all here today."

I look at the clock and see that time really is ticking on. I wonder where Rob is now. Is he really coming to take his children away? I'm starting to feel suspicious that it was just an empty threat. It's a long way from Gloucester and would his mum really want him to do this? Who knows? She maybe feels very protective of her son and would go to any lengths to support him. It's very possible that he is as manipulative of her as he is his wife and that his mum has no idea what he's like to Natalie.

My thoughts turn to my own parents. I pick up my phone. "I won't be long," I say and go upstairs to our room, which feels very cool in contrast with the lounge.

"Hello?" Mum says and I see her face come into view and then Dad's too.

"We're on the deck!" he exclaims and I'm treated to the view of the deck of the ship, and a couple of other people sitting on sun loungers, although it is clearly night-time. The couple raise their glasses and smile. "Merry Christmas!"

"Merry Christmas!" I laugh.

"That's Sheila and Mike," Mum says. "They're our cruise buddies. Now, how's your day been?"

"It's still going strong!" I smile. "I just wanted to say thanks to you and Dad for helping us out. And for not minding about us sharing out the presents."

"Oh it's no bother at all. Our pleasure. Those poor children. That poor young woman."

"I know."

"We'd gone a bit overboard to be honest – touch wood, shouldn't say that on a cruise ship – and as I'm sure Sam will tell you, I couldn't even remember what everything was. Did it all work out?"

"Perfectly!" I smile. "I won't stay on long now and it looks like you're having lots of fun anyway."

"Oh yes, we are."

"Oh no we're not!" I hear Sheila and Mike chorus off-camera before bursting into guffaws.

Mum smiles. "We may have had a drink or two."

"Really? I couldn't tell."

"You enjoy the rest of your day now, love…"

"I will, but hang on Mum…"

"Yes?"

"I forgot to ask you… about Nigel. Did he get to his niece's OK?"

"Oh no, well yes, he did, but she was going to her in-laws' so he only stopped up there for a night. I think he said to your dad he was coming back to Cornwall, to have that dinner at the Bay he'd booked. Bless him."

"On his own?"

"Well, yes, I suppose so."

My mind flies to the mobile home I'd spotted earlier. It must be his.

"Thanks, Mum. Enjoy the rest of your day."

"We will. Happy Christmas, Alice."

185

"Happy Christmas, love." Dad finally gets the phone away from Mum.

"Happy Christmas, Dad. I love you."

"Love you too," they say in sync with each other and then they are gone. But I don't have time to miss them. I have something else to do.

I dash down the stairs, putting my head round the lounge door. "Have you seen Sam?" I ask Natalie and then I hear a lot of clanging about in the kitchen. "Don't worry, I think I know where he is!"

I go through to see him. "Sam…"

"Yes?" He spins round. He knows when I'm going to ask him for something. In my robin apron, with his sleeves rolled up, he looks very lovely.

"Do you think we might be able to feed one more?"

"What? Who?"

I tell him about Nigel. "I'm going to get him!" I am buoyed up, full of Christmas spirit.

"What if it's not him?" asks Sam. "Or what if it is, and he doesn't want to come?"

"It's him," I say. "It must be. And of course he'll want to come and celebrate with us. Who wouldn't?"

I kiss Sam, grab my keys, and I'm off and out through the door into the night.

23

The weather outside is frightful. In the time we've been back, the rain has really set in and I have to put my wipers on top speed to keep my vision clear. No sooner have I turned out of our road than my phone starts ringing. In the hands-free holder, it displays Julie's name. Damn, I was meant to call her earlier. I pull over to the side of the road and accept the call. She's on video and has Zinnia on her lap, clutching the cuddly bunny we sent for her.

"Happy Christmas my friend!" says Julie. "Where the heck are you?"

"I'm in the car."

"I can see that!" She rolls her eyes. "But why are you in the car and not cosying up with your loved ones?"

"It's a long story," I say.

"I'm all ears... but first, talking of ears, Zinnia what do you have to say to Alice?"

"Thank you Alice! I love my bunny!"

"You are very welcome, Zinnie. Holly wants you to call her Holly. But you can choose your own name."

"Holly is perfect," Zinnia says, sounding very grown up. And is that a twang of a Canadian accent I can hear?

"Well, have a think about it. And if you decide on Holly, you can tell my Holly. She'll be so happy! Maybe you can have a video call with her and Ben tomorrow?"

"Yes!"

"Good girl," says Julie and she helps Zinnia slide off her lap. "Now I need to hear about Alice's Christmas Day." She waits a moment, presumably till Zinnia is out of earshot. "What's going on?"

I pause, wondering where to begin, and I start with Natalie, and Rob, and him leaving them with no gas, electricity, or Christmas presents.

"Bloody hell," says Julie, whose face has become increasingly animated and disbelieving as I've told her what's happened.

"I know. And Natalie's at our house wondering if he's about to turn up any minute and take the children back up to Gloucester."

"Poor woman," Julie says.

"I know," I sigh. "And I feel like I've been a bit shit to be honest. But it's because I miss you," I say pathetically.

"Don't blame your rubbish behaviour on me!" Julie laughs. "But I miss you too. So much. But Alice…"

"Yes?"

"If Natalie's at your house, why are you sitting in your car?"

"Ah yes, I almost forgot that part." I fill her in on Nigel's appearance at Mum and Dad's, and how I'd spotted what must be his mobile home on the Island car park. "I know he parked there before, and he was being quite cunning, just stopping the one night… come to think of it–" I say, remembering our meal out with David and Martin. Was that really only two days ago? It feels like weeks – "I think he may have been parked up on the Three Barrels car park the other day. Bloody hell, I can't believe I didn't think of it then."

"So you're going down to a strange van on a quiet car park in the pouring rain and you're planning to do what…?"

"Invite him up to ours, of course!"

"Alice, are you sure it's him?"

"Pretty sure," I say, doubt creeping in.

"Right. Here's what you're going to do. You and I are going to keep this call going. You're going to drive down to the car park… put your phone in your pocket, I don't want my beautiful face distracting you from your driving… and you can keep me connected while you find out if it really is Nigel."

"OK," I say, wondering what on earth Julie can do from Canada, if there is a problem. I suppose she can alert Sam. So I do as I'm told and I put the phone in my pocket. I can hear Julie singing *Let it Snow*. "Shut up, you idiot!" I call. "You may have a beautiful face but your voice is awful."

"Very rude," Julie says, "but I suppose there's a compliment in there somewhere so I'll let you off. Where are you now?"

I talk Julie through my journey and she oohs and ahhs and reminisces about the pasties from the bakery on the hill, and the Christmas lights on the harbour. It's almost like having her in the car with me.

"You'll have to come back and visit in the summer," I say.

"I think we will."

As I approach the Island car park, I start to feel a little bit nervous. What if Julie's right and it's not Nigel? I mean, I can't remember his registration plate or the make and model of his mobile home. It's just this one seems familiar, and it all seems to add up…

I park the car and Julie says, "Where are we now?"

"In the car park," I say. "I'm going to get out of the car now so be quiet, OK? I don't want to scare him off."

"He's not a stray dog," says Julie.

"No, but… look, just no singing, OK?" The rain has died down a bit, I'm pleased to note.

"Fine," she huffs, and I step out into the festive Christmas drizzle.

Tiptoeing carefully round puddles, the hems of my trousers soaking up the rain as I go, I feel my heart thudding as I approach the mobile home. The lights are still on and I can hear loud voices. Does Nigel have guests? Or is it not Nigel at all? Or is it… well it sounds like Del Boy, so I'll assume it's the TV.

I step up bravely to the door. I knock. The sound of the TV is immediately gone. Even Julie is quiet. The door opens slowly…

"Nigel!" I say, my relief evident. "I knew it was you."

He looks surprised to see me and puzzled by the cheering sounds coming from my pocket. "Alice?"

"Nigel! Are you OK?"

"I'm fine. But why are you out here in the rain?"

"I-I came to invite you to dinner."

"What? How did you know I was here?"

"I spotted your van earlier. And was that you the other day in the Three Barrels car park?" The words are flying out of me, I'm feeling very clever for tracking him down.

"Well yes but, well I've already had my dinner."

The table at the Bay. Of course.

"Was it good?" I ask lamely.

"Delicious," he says. "One of the best Christmas dinners I've had."

I sense something in him; not pride exactly, but dignity. That's it. He does not want my sympathy, or my charity.

"Well look," I say, "we're not doing a traditional Christmas dinner." I explain about how it's all a bit mix and match. "And we've got some friends over too, who had a – a power cut, and it's all very low key and informal, but we'd love you to come and join us."

Nigel looks at me, considering. I feel like Julie is holding her breath, waiting for his decision. "Alright," he says slowly. "Thank you."

There is more cheering from my pocket. "It's my friend," I say.

"Oh right," says Nigel, looking at me strangely. I imagine he's wondering if he should have accepted an invitation from a soaked-through woman who thinks she's got one of her friends in her pocket. "Hang on though, Alice. Can I just get a couple of things together?"

"Of course. Listen, do you mind if I go back to the car? It's the one with the lights on over there. Just come across when you're ready."

"I will!" He smiles at me, looking delighted now. "I'll be right with you."

I retrace my steps, not minding the puddles. My feet and legs are soaked anyway. I splash along merrily and get back into the car, replacing my phone in its holder.

"Told you it was him!" I say to Julie.

"Alright, smartarse. Keep me connected though, just till he's in the car, OK?"

"OK… he's coming." My heart sinks slightly at the sight of Nigel with what appears to be a huge bag under his arm. Does he think I've invited him to stay the night? Then again, I suppose he can. There's the spare room. Natalie and the kids could have the lounge again... *Come on Alice, it's Christmas!* I tell myself.

Nigel opens the passenger door. "Mind if I put this in the boot?" he says, already moving towards it.

I turn to Julie and we share a look. When Nigel gets into the car, I say, "This is Julie," gesturing at the phone.

"Hello love!" he says. "I remember you. Least, I think I do. Weren't you two joined at the hip?"

"Yes!" says Julie. "I think I remember you too!" Does she actually? It doesn't really matter because Nigel looks so pleased.

"Julie's in Canada now," I explain, "and she called me on the way down here. She wanted to make sure I wasn't just knocking on the door of some strange man."

"Very sensible," says Nigel. "I could have been anyone."

His accent is familiar to both me and Julie, reminding us of the place we grew up.

"Are you doing a tour, Nigel?" Julie asks.

"Something like that."

"I'm going to start driving back. If you don't mind. But you two keep chatting if you like." I turn the phone screen towards Nigel. And chat they do, and then I hear Julie's mum, Cherry, saying hello, and that she also remembers Nigel, and now he is grinning from ear to ear.

"It's not been the same since Phil and Sue moved down here," he says with some regret. "They were good friends to me, I wanted to come and treat them, but I should have known they'd already be booked up. I've lived as a bachelor too long."

"Oh Nigel, don't worry, I've been on my own a long time too. I know what you mean," says Cherry.

And the pair of them strike up a conversation, realising

they have other friends and places in common, and must only live about five miles from each other – "When I'm not on the road!" says Nigel, making himself sound quite the seasoned traveller – as I drive back up through town and into our street.

"Here we are," I say.

"I'd better go," says Nigel, moving to end the call.

"Hang on!" I laugh, taking the phone out of the holder. "Happy Christmas, Cherry." I smile at the sight of Julie's mum, who looks so happy to be with her family.

"And to you, Alice love. Have a lovely evening. You too, Nigel. Maybe I'll bump into you sometime."

"Maybe you will." Nigel can be quite the charmer, it would seem.

Once Cherry is gone, Julie's face appears again, rolling her eyes. I laugh. "I'll call you tomorrow. Give my love to everyone there, and have an amazing Christmas."

"Will do. Love you."

"Love you too."

I turn to Nigel. "Right, you'd better come and meet the gang." I feel like I've just stepped into an Enid Blyton novel.

Inside, there is a Christmas disco going on in the lounge, Sam partnering Holly, Ben partnering Courtney, and Bobby and his mum dancing together.

"Everyone!" I say. "This is Nigel."

"Hello Nigel!" they chorus.

Natalie hugs Bobby and comes across. "Hello Nigel, nice to meet you," she says, shaking his hand.

"Nigel, good to see you again," says Sam. "Shall I take your coat?"

The children are less interested in this older stranger but

I feel the warmth of Sam's and Natalie's greetings seeping into him. "Yes, although… can I just get my bag from the car?" he asks.

"Moving in?" Sam laughs when he sees the size of Nigel's bag.

Potentially awkward, I think. I haven't had a chance to ask Nigel if he's intending to stay over.

"Nothing like that Sam, all will be revealed." Nigel taps the side of his nose.

"It's not that kind of party," Sam tries a bit of banter and it goes down very well.

Nigel laughs loudly and slaps Sam on the back. "I should think not, too!"

Natalie pulls me gently aside. She is smiling. "Rob messaged me."

Oh no, I think. *Please don't say you're taking him back.*

"He's not coming down. Says the weather's too bad."

"It's a bit late in the day, isn't it?"

"Yeah, I think he was just trying to keep me scared."

"So do you want to stay here tonight? And really until we get things sorted with your utilities?" I very much doubt that will be happening on Boxing Day.

"Would that be OK? I am sorr—"

"You're learning!" I laugh. "Of course that's OK."

Sam leads the way into the lounge, Nigel and Natalie following on. I stop in the hallway for just a moment, listening to their voices. Sam asking Nigel about his van, Natalie telling a joke to the kids. The resulting laughter. This is far from the Christmas I was expecting, but I love it. I really do.

24

Sam has been very busy all round, moving apparently seamlessly from organising our second round of present-opening to making sure there is plenty of food for all.

An array of timers sits on the kitchen worktop, alongside the air fryer and the toastie maker, as Courtney apparently only wants a cheese toastie. I look at Sam's list of what is cooking and when it's ready.

"You sit down now," I say to him. "I'll take it from here."

"Erm…"

"Yes OK, I can see you've done everything there is to do! But we need some more chairs. In fact, we probably need another table really, if we all want to sit together."

"Maybe we could borrow from Natalie?" Sam suggests.

"Good idea, I'll go and ask her."

In the lounge all is relatively quiet. The children are in various positions of relaxation on the settee, Holly leaning against Ben and sucking her thumb. Courtney too seems to have taken a liking to Ben and she is sitting leaning close to his other side, her little knees bent up under her chin. Bobby sits next to her, lost in whatever it is they're watching.

"A rose between two thorns, eh Ben?" I say.

He looks at me. "What?"

"Never mind!" I laugh and turn to Natalie, who is listening to a story Nigel is telling her. "Sorry to interrupt, but would we maybe be able to borrow the table and chairs from your house?"

"Oh my god of course, I should have thought of that, sorry." Natalie practically springs to her feet.

"Don't worry! And remember... no more saying sorry. I might have to get you an apology jar."

"Sorr... anyway, yes, let's go. Do you need anything else? Tablecloth? Napkins?"

"Actually, yes, that would be great," I say, eyeing up our table. "We might need to shift the furniture around a bit to make some space..."

"I can do that!" volunteers Nigel. "Unless you need a hand carrying things over?"

"I think we'll manage, thank you Nigel. If you can shift the settee away from the dining area though, that would be great. You might have to ask the kids to move."

"No need for that!" Nigel says. "Who wants a ride on the sofa?" he asks the four children, who all answer a delighted yes. Ben tries not to sound too delighted but I can see from his face that he is.

Nigel stands and begins to try to move the settee, pretending to struggle and hold his back. He has all the children giggling.

Natalie and I smile at each other and make our escape. Thankfully, it's stopped raining and as we step outside I can see the moon just behind the rooftops, peeping over at us as we walk down the street to the only house not shining with light.

Once we get inside, Natalie reaches automatically towards the light switch and then remembers.

"We'll help you get sorted, don't worry," I say, switching on my phone torch. "Now, show me the way!"

Of course she doesn't need to really, as her house is laid out identically to ours. Into the lounge on the left and through to the dining area. She has two tables; one of them is at a low level, presumably for the children.

"Should we take that one?" Natalie suggests. "We could have an adults' table and kids' table. That's what we always did at family parties when I was little."

"Oh yes that's a great idea! It'll be like a throwback to the eighties… Nineties?" I suggest, remembering Natalie is younger than me.

"I've got a Christmas tablecloth somewhere too, I know it's in one of the drawers in the kitchen…"

Her suggestion of a kids' table has me telling her about my suggestion to Mum of starting a retro catering company, hosting dinner parties and buffets.

"Oh my god, I love that idea!" says Natalie. "I'd love to come up with something like that. You're really smart, Alice."

Never comfortable with that kind of compliment, I shrug it off. "I think it's just a product of working with all these amazing little companies," I say. "I've met a lot of inspirational people, and Shona's really teaching me to think around things, to make campaigns original and fresh. It's obviously got my creativity flowing!"

"I'd love to run my own business," Natalie says as she rummages in a drawer. "I really used to like work, getting involved in events. It could be so stressful, but it was amazing when things went well. And actually, in a weird way I liked it when things went wrong because it was a bit of pressure. A challenge, you know?"

"Well, if you want to you can have the dinner party idea! I don't think Mum will go for it really. And I am an absolutely lousy cook, as anyone will happily tell you, so I know it's not for me."

"Oh – found it!" Natalie says, holding up a pristine tablecloth in the light of her phone. She resumes her search. "I've got some matching napkins too… but what I was going to say was that you wouldn't need to be able to cook. You can source the food from somebody else. You could just manage the whole event. I bet it's not that different to what you used to do at Amethi."

"No," I muse, "I guess not. But it seems to me like it's struck a chord with you. And you know what, I do like my work these days. And it's flexible enough that I can always do whatever I need to for Holly, whether it's popping into school or taking her to clinic. Natalie, if you like the idea, and you would like to think some more about it, you should go for it, honestly! It's my Christmas gift to you!"

"Oh Alice," she straightens up and hugs me. "When I thought about this Christmas I had absolutely no idea that it would turn like this. I mean, only this morning I thought it was over. I thought the kids would hate me and Rob would come and take them away, and…"

Almost at the exact moment she says Rob's name, we hear a car outside.

"What was that?" she asks and I see the fear manifest on her face.

"Turn that off," I say quietly, switching the light off on my own phone and gently taking hers in order to do the same.

"Sshhh," I say as quietly as I can, "let's just listen. It may be somebody calling in at Jill and Raymond's."

But the headlights are shining directly in through the frosted glass of Natalie's front door, filtering into the kitchen. My own heart starts to race. Clearly Rob had told her he wasn't coming so that she'd be here when he arrived. And maybe he was just enjoying toying with her a little more anyway. I try to control my breathing, exhaling slowly and very quietly. There is something about being in the dark that makes this whole situation much more terrifying. Just when we thought it was safe to relax.

A shadow obscures the beams of light. We hear a knock on the door, and somebody tries the handle.

"I left the keys in the lock, inside," Natalie whispers. "Habit. Rob always made me do it when he was away. In case anyone wanted to break in."

It sounds to me like he was playing with her emotions and building up fear; creating a lack of trust in the world outside their home. It's backfired on him now. But it seems like he's not giving up.

We hear the side gate go and we hold our collective breath. Should we sneak into the hallway, I wonder, imagining him shining a torch on us.

It's just Rob, I tell myself. He may be a bastard but he's not a murderer. Then again, I think with a chill, isn't it said that most murders of women are committed by partners or ex-partners? *Pull yourself together, Alice! Time to be strong for Natalie.*

"Crouch down," I hiss. "We'll get behind the kitchen counters and then he won't be able to see us."

"OK," she says, her eyes wide.

We crouch together and I immediately regret it. My legs

are not what they used to be. I doubt my ability to maintain this position for too long.

A beam of light sweeps the room, skimming the counter tops. Natalie is shaking. I put my arm round her.

"Natalie?"

That isn't a man's voice.

Natalie looks up. "Mum?"

Still trembling, Natalie stands. It takes me a moment to make sense of what's happening and then I stand too.

"It's your mum!" I burst out laughing, unable to control my relief. And Natalie is laughing too, and we're holding onto each other for support.

"Natalie? Is that you?" The figure at the window is peering through. Natalie rushes to the back door, unlocking it and letting her mum in.

The pair of them hug with such ferocity that I could cry.

"What are you doing here?" Natalie asks. "It's Christmas."

"Well exactly. And what's Christmas without you and Bobby and Courtney?" Natalie's mum looks around now, her eyes seeking her grandchildren but finding only me. I smile, though I am still feeling wobbly.

"Mum," Natalie says, "this is my friend Alice. Alice, this is my mum, Becky."

I feel a swelling of pride at the words 'my friend'.

"Oh Alice, I've heard about you. Natalie always says how kind you are."

I look at my feet. I don't think I deserve that for the way I've treated her these last few months.

"Well," I say, "I've heard a lot about you too. How long has it taken you to get here?"

"Only about eight hours!" Becky laughs. "Not counting comfort breaks. I borrowed the car from Dennis."

"Oh Dennis! Our old neighbour," Natalie explains to me. "I miss him! But oh my god, Mum, I can't believe you've spent your Christmas Day driving down here."

"Well of course I have. You're my daughter, aren't you? I'd do anything for you."

And that has me. It has all of us in fact, and Natalie and Becky hug again, their tears mingling, and I stand there like a spare part, almost wanting to join in but thinking that might be very weird seeing as Becky's only just met me.

"You're going to have to join us for Christmas dinner," I say instead.

"Oh, really? I couldn't…"

"Of course you could!" I exclaim. "Over at our house. That's where your beautiful grandchildren are! We only came back for an extra table and some chairs."

"Well let me carry some," says Becky.

"Sure," I say, and the three of us gather what we need, Natalie locking the back door and letting us out of the front.

"We're like the three wise women," I say as we parade down the street. "Bringing gifts of tablecloths, napkins and chair…"

"That's terrible, Alice," Natalie calls over her shoulder.

"Yes, it is, sorry."

Sam opens the door to let us through and barely bats an eyelid at the fact we now have another guest. I introduce him and Becky, and then on hearing their grandma's voice, Bobby and Courtney rush through to the hallway. There are more hugs, more tears.

"Shall I go and get the presents?" Becky asks quietly, when everything's settled down.

Natalie and I look at each other.

"To be honest, Mum, I think that we might have had

201

enough presents for today," says Natalie. "Can we save them for tomorrow?"

"Of course, love. Of course."

I wonder where Becky is staying tonight and prepare myself for another unexpected guest. But first, dinner… it's been a long day and I'm starving.

Becky and Natalie lay out the new tablecloth and napkins and the kids love the idea of having their own table next to the adults. "It's like when you and Tom were kids!" Becky says. Natalie looks at me and smiles.

Sam and I bring through plate after plate of food for people to just help themselves, and from under a small silver serving dome he reveals a cheese toastie just for Courtney. She claps her little hands with glee.

Nigel produces two bottles of chilled champagne from his bag. He opens one after the other with a flourish. "I don't think just one's going to last very long," he says. We toast each other and the children lift their cups of lemonade, the boys bashing them against each other's until we have to tell them to stop.

When Holly has piled up her plate, Natalie asks if she can see her insulin pump and Holly is delighted to show her, and then Becky wants to see, and both of them tell her about Tom and what a great strong young man he is now and how diabetes hasn't stopped him from doing anything. Holly listens, delighted at the attention and wanting to meet Tom, who I know is already achieving hero status in her mind.

"Alright?" Sam asks quietly, and I do have to take a moment to compose myself from watching this scene play out. I would never hide Holly's diabetes away from anyone but to have people filling her with confidence and

202

positivity about it is such a joy. I take a big gulp of my champagne and Nigel tops up my glass.

"Plenty more where that came from, Alice. And may I just say," he raises his voice a little, "a huge thank you to our generous hosts? To Alice and Sam." He lifts his glass and Becky, Natalie and all the children follow suit.

Sam and I look at each other, embarrassed but pleased.

"It's a pleasure to have you all here," Sam says, his cheeks reddening a little. "Now tuck in!"

And we do. And incredibly, those piles of food in the centre of the table diminish rapidly. Poor Becky hasn't eaten since breakfast, aside from a bag of crisps from Exeter services, so she's famished. Nobody seems to mind that it isn't your usual Christmas dinner, and the champagne is followed by red wine, which helps to keep the conversation oiled and flowing.

At some point, I stop while everyone else is chatting. Becky is talking to Nigel, Sam is talking to Natalie. The four children are talking either to, with, or over each other but whatever it is, none of them seem to mind. I sit back in my chair and just take it all in for a moment. This day was meant to be for just the four of us – five of us, I remind myself, leaning back to ruffle the fur of Meg, who is lying behind my chair. Now look at this room. It's a total mess, with wrapping paper everywhere and the detritus of nine Christmas crackers – not to mention plates and cups and god knows what else – but it is warm and full and fun, and everything that Christmas should be.

And actually, when dinner is done and after we have all spent a good ten minutes patting our overly full bellies and exclaiming how stuffed we are, it is all-hands-on-deck and we soon have everything cleared away. Natalie and her mum are quite a team in the kitchen and I see how organised and efficient Natalie is. Sam makes some coffee and tea, and I stand by feeling quite redundant as Becky and Natalie insist they have washing and drying down to a fine art.

"Come on Meg," I say, when Sam has handed me a coffee. "Shall we go outside?"

Not so long ago, Meg would have been on her feet and at the back door like a flash. Now, she stands up slowly and plods across, like she's doing me a favour. In a way, she is. I open the door and follow her out. It's colder now than it has been on the previous evenings this week, and I'm pleased to see the stars have joined the moon, which has curved its way up high now.

Meg pads around on the wet grass and I hold my mug between my two hands, leaning back against the wall. I feel very well fed and pleasantly merry from the wine. It's nice to have a few moments to let everything settle around me, before I go back in to join the fun.

In time, I hear Holly calling my name.

"Coming!" I shout and I look at Meg. "Shall we?"

What do you think I've been waiting for? Meg's expression seems to say.

"Come on then," I follow Meg inside, where she collapses into her bed with relief. She'll be tired tomorrow.

I go through to the lounge, readying myself to be the perfect host. I was not expecting the sight that greets me.

A screen has been put up against the wall and on it is a picture of me, when I was about seven years old. Donning what I remember was a particular favourite dress of mine, some thick red tights, and a Christmas cracker hat.

"What's this?" I laugh.

"It's Nigel's!" exclaims Ben. "A side show."

"Slide show!" Sam laughs. "Look, Alice. Nigel's got loads of pictures from your old house."

"And look at Granny and Grandad! They had coloured hair!" laughs Holly.

"They did, didn't they?" I say, walking up to the screen. "I can't believe this!" I say to Nigel.

"Yes well I've been doing a lot of sorting out of stuff and I thought I'd bring these for your mum and dad. But they're not here of course, and when you turned up earlier, I just had to bring them up here for you to see. There's some happy memories in here." He pats the box of slides. "Your mum and dad were very good to me, Alice. Always made me feel very welcome."

It's not the first time he's said this but it really begins to hit home how much my parents' kind inclusivity must have meant to him.

"And your mum was a lovely little girl," Nigel says to Ben and Holly.

"And now she's so old!" Ben says, which has Bobby in stitches.

I pretend to cuff Ben round the ear but I slide down onto the arm of the seat next to him and I am gratified when he snuggles into me, and we watch Nigel's show together. There are pictures of me and my parents through the years. Even, embarrassingly, evidence of my solo shows played out in front of the patio windows.

But some of those images just bring my memories flooding back. Even the sight of our old fake Christmas tree with its cheap and cheerful baubles and tinsel. And there are pictures from summer parties in the garden and even a day out to the North Wales coast, with my grandma. I smile to see her image there on the big screen and I want to go and touch it. It's funny how Nigel had slipped from my mind over the years but he was present in our lives quite a lot when I was little. I suppose children don't necessarily notice and appreciate these things, taking people's presence for granted.

"Do you like them, Alice?" Nigel asks.

"I do. I really do." I feel slightly embarrassed that everyone else has had to sit through a load of pictures of me and my family, but nobody seems to mind, or at least they are too polite to say if they do.

"Well you hang onto them, to show Sue and Phil, and I'll be back sometime next year. I can pick them up then."

"Are you sure?"

"Of course!"

"Thank you, Nigel, they will love to see these."

I feel shattered all of a sudden, and it seems I am not the only one. Courtney is nearly asleep in her grandma's arms, and I realise we haven't solved the problem of where everyone is going to sleep.

"I've got an idea," I say. "Why don't we pack some bags, Sam, and me, you, Ben and Holly can go down to Mum and Dad's? Nigel, you can walk down to town with us. Then you four can stay here," I say to Natalie. "As long as you don't mind letting Meg out in the morning. And giving her some breakfast."

"Oh we couldn't turf you out Alice," protests Natalie.

"You're not, I promise." In all honesty, I like the idea. Seeing all those pictures of the past has me missing Mum and Dad and it seems like I might feel closer to them if I'm at their house. It won't do Natalie and her mum any harm to have some time with just Bobby and Courtney either, and I could be in with a chance of making it to the Boxing Day swim if the beach is not so far away. I might even persuade Sam to join me, though that may be a bit too optimistic.

"That's fine by me," says Nigel. "A bit of fresh air would do me good."

"Then that's settled," I say. "Here, Natalie, let me show you where everything is while I get some things together."

We don't need much, Mum and Dad are already well set up for having the kids to stay over. Natalie lies on the spare bed as I pack two bags. "I thought this was going to be the worst Christmas ever, Alice, but in a weird way it might have been the best. One of the best, at least. Thank you."

"Honestly, truly, it's been our pleasure. You can have us to you next year!"

Natalie opens her mouth then realises I'm teasing. We both know that there is a lot of time before next Christmas. Who knows where she'll be then? I do very much hope that she will still be in Cornwall.

Our goodbyes done, Courtney clinging to Natalie with eyes half-closed, Sam, Nigel and I begin the walk down to town. Sam has Ben on his shoulders, which is no mean feat these days, and I am carrying Holly. The streets are peaceful and I think of the quiet harbour nestling down in the crook of the town's elbow. Boats will be rocking gently, masts creaking and chains sliding and clanking. I suppose the pubs will still be full but it always feels more gentle and good-natured at Christmas somehow; it's a different crowd of people who come out for a post-dinner or post-walk beer or wine or whisky to round the day off.

I'm grateful to be heading towards a comfy bed in a house I love dearly. As we approach, we say our goodnights to Nigel and he thanks us again. I feel a wave of fondness towards him. "Thank you," I say, "for your company and for that blast from the past with all those slides. I love them and I know Mum and Dad will. And you know, you say how good they always were to you but I am quite sure you were just as good a friend to them."

In the light of the streetlamp, he looks almost set to cry but instead he just hugs me. "You were a good girl then Alice, and you are now. You just carry on as you are and you won't go far wrong."

And off he goes, down the street and on towards the harbour. He cuts a solitary figure as he passes under the next streetlight and I feel my heart reaching out to him. I don't want him to be alone, even if he is used to it. But Sam takes my hand and gently pulls me into Mum and Dad's house. He kisses me in the hallway as the kids run through the different rooms, switching on the lights and laughing as they chase each other.

I consider all the times Sam and I have stood in this exact spot and shared a kiss. He may be thinking along the same lines because he looks intently at me before kissing me again.

"Happy Christmas, Alice."

25

I wake up in a strange yet familiar space and my head is so fuzzy it takes me a moment to remember I am in Mum and Dad's spare bedroom. Sam is still asleep and I stretch my legs out luxuriously, enjoying the warm, velvety darkness that the blackout curtains provide.

I sneak across to the window and pull the curtains back slightly to see that it is already full daylight out there. We are at the back of the house and the window overlooks my parents' suntrap garden, complete with the same furniture that has been there since David owned this place. Behind the back garden wall is the little alleyway that leads down to town. A seagull perches on the wall, ruffling up its feathers and then raising its face towards the sun, emitting a loud cry before shaking out its wings and taking to the sky. I look across the rooftops, rewarded by a glimpse of the glistening sea. It's a beautiful day out there.

A glance at my watch tells me it is well after 8am. The children must still be fast asleep after all the excitement and what turned out to be a late night. I sigh contentedly, moving my head gently side to side then up and down, shrugging my shoulders and feeling a satisfying click.

Boxing Day. The best of all the festive days when you get to my age.

"Come back to bed!" I hear Sam's voice and I turn, pulling back the curtains a little further so that a stripe of sparkling, dusty air opens up and my usually beautiful golden Sam squints and grimaces like a gargoyle against the sudden brightness.

"What time is it?" he asks.

"Nearly half eight."

"No sign of the kids?"

"No!" I say, trying to suppress my smile. It's not that I don't want to see them but these days I do very much appreciate anything that resembles a lie-in.

Sam lifts his phone. I know he's checking Holly's numbers.

"Everything OK?"

"Looks like it. Now come back to bed," he says again, pulling back the covers. I do as I'm bid and I climb in beside him. He pulls the duvet up, moving onto his side to face me and shuffling an arm underneath me. He strokes my back. "Alright?"

"Yes," I smile and kiss him. "You?"

"Yes. I mean, I'm knackered, but this is it now, isn't it? We can relax a bit."

"Apart from a birthday party for fifteen kids tomorrow, yes!" I laugh as he groans. "Just be grateful somebody else is doing the entertaining. All we have to do is make the sandwiches and pack some party bags. But that is not for now." I kiss him again then I rest my head against him. "It's not been the worst Christmas, has it?"

"No, not by a long way. I've enjoyed it." Sam's voice reverberates through his chest. I can hear his heart thudding away reassuringly as well.

"And it was nice, wasn't it, having unexpected guests?" I am aware I kind of made all that happen without much consultation with Sam. But I also know what a kind-hearted, generous man he is and that he is unlikely to begrudge these things.

"It was really nice," he reassures me. "That's what Christmas is about, isn't it?"

"And presents," I remind him.

"Oh yes, and presents. That's the most important bit."

We both fall silent for a while. My eyes feel heavy and achy. I would like nothing more than to stay in bed and sleep in my husband's arms all day. But I know it won't be long before our children wake up and they'll need us to get up with them, be with them. Help them both make breakfast and help Holly with all her kit. Which makes these few moments – however long we've got – all the more precious.

"It's been a busy week," I observe.

"Just a bit. Bloody hell. I was thinking actually, it's been a bit like *A Christmas Carol*. We've had Christmas Past with Nigel and all his slides. And Christmas Yet to Come, at Paul and Shona's house. Did you think it was a bit sad?"

"What?"

"I don't know… seeing them with grown-up children, and ageing parents. I know it's hard work when the kids are little but one day they're going to be too old for Father Christmas and waking up early. They'll be off to the pub on Christmas Eve and staying in bed late nursing their hangovers. And your mum and my mum will be sitting in opposite corners of the room sniping at each other."

"They won't!" I laugh. "But I know what you mean." I consider a future where Ben and Holly don't need us in the way they do now. And where they might bring partners home, and those partners come to mean more to them than we do. "But it doesn't have to be like that, does it? We could travel the world."

"Go cruising like Sue and Phil?"

"That sounds wrong!" I laugh. "But why not? I love being parents, more than anything in the world, but I do miss our times together, just the two of us."

"Me too," Sam says, kissing the top of my head.

"But I also can't imagine not being like this. A family of four. Five," I correct myself, as always thinking of lovely Meg back at home, which then makes me think of Natalie. I hope they're all OK. I hope Natalie slept and felt safe. Even if Rob had turned up during the night I doubt he'd have thought to look for them at our house.

"We're so lucky," I say, leaning up on my elbow and looking at Sam.

"We are. And that's the present, isn't it?" Sam smiles at me and looks away almost shyly, as he often does when he goes all earnest. "We're so lucky with where we are and everything we have. We might prefer some alternative situations. We miss people... we definitely wish Holly wasn't diabetic. But despite that, we are so lucky. And Christmas might not have been what we thought it was going to be. There was a lot more drama, for a start. But it all worked out. And I know that Nigel appreciated it. Poor bloke."

"I know. He must be lonely."

"He is," Sam confirms. "It's obvious, isn't it? But I had a good chat with him you know, and there's even more going on than that."

"Oh?"

"Yeah. He's having a few health issues. He didn't go into details but he said he's still having tests for whatever it is. I gather he's worried it's something serious. It may all be OK still but he knows he's not been well for a while and he said he was too scared to go to the doctor at first. I suppose it's even more daunting when you're alone. So anyway, he's seizing the moment, he said; taking this time to try and see the people who have been important in his life. He's got more tests coming up in the new year so he's using his couple of weeks' grace to try and see the people who matter."

"No!" I'm shocked. "That's so sad." I'd just thought Nigel was living a single man's life, trundling nostalgically here and there in glorious, oblivious bachelorhood, calling upon whoever he fancied, not stopping to think that people might have other things going on in their lives.

"I know." Sam touches my cheek with the back of his hand. "But it might yet come good. There might be nothing to worry about, or it could be something they can put right. But he's taking the opportunity to do this while he knows that he can."

"Should I tell Mum and Dad?" I ask.

"No, don't worry. I suggested to him that he comes back at New Year. They'll be home then, won't they? I thought that they'd be up for having a drink with him. Do you think that's OK?" Sam looks suddenly doubtful.

"I think that is more than OK. I am sure they'll be happy to have another chance to spend some time with him. And maybe he can show them all those slides himself."

"Just as long as we don't have to sit through another show. No offence," says Sam, "I mean it was lovely to see those pictures but it's a bit like having to look at somebody else's holiday snaps, isn't it?"

"I guess it is," I laugh, although I wouldn't mind looking at those slides again. "So anyway…. we've covered past, present and future, just like in the book. The question I'm left with, Sam, is this —"

He's a step ahead of me. "I have been giving this some thought and I didn't really want to say…"

"Shit," I say disbelievingly but I can see he's right. I've not been the most cheery person of late. I've been tired and grumpy about having too much to do and Sam not being at home so much, and I've made it quite obvious how much I'm missing Julie, and Amethi, and resenting working for Shona, even though I know it's really a tremendous blessing. I've been insular and inward-looking and I certainly haven't been welcoming to Natalie. I was disparaging about Nigel and secretly annoyed at Mum and Dad for going away – yet also secretly pleased that Karen was not going to be here. I have been distinctly lacking in Christmas spirit.

But gradually everything has changed. I have seen the error of my ways, and I really hope that the last day or so has seen me starting to put things right.

"It's me, isn't it? I'm Ebenezer Scrooge."

"You are," Sam agrees. "But don't worry, I still love you."

Not long after this disturbing revelation we hear footsteps up above. Ben and Holly have been sharing the bed in my old attic room and we brace ourselves as we hear the pair of them galloping down the stairs and pushing the door open. Ben appears first.

"You, boy," I say. "What day is it?"

"It's Boxing Day, Mum."

He rolls his eyes, he can't believe I've forgotten. Then,

followed closely by Holly, he jumps onto our bed and the two of them squeeze between me and Sam. Our eyes meet over the top of our children's heads. Our moment will come again I think, but for now this is where we are. This is our Christmas Present.

Epilogue

Eventually, we cannot ignore our rumbling stomachs and we head downstairs to raid Mum and Dad's cupboards. There's a disappointing selection to be had; dry granola and muesli, with no milk in the fridge. I check the freezer for bread and instead find a selection of Danish pastries.

"We'll replace these," I say, switching on the oven.

"Of course," says Sam, turning on the coffee machine. "Why is it that even now we're supposedly adults, it feels OK to just help ourselves to our parents' stuff?"

"And why is their stuff so much nicer than ours?"

"We're missing a trick somewhere," Sam says.

I'm especially glad now that we persuaded Dad to have the Christmas tree up as it feels very festive in their front room. I am tempted to light a fire but that feels a bit too cheeky. If we end up staying another night, which I guess we may have to – it's unlikely Natalie will have any joy with the utility companies today – we can get one going tonight.

I settle the children down in front of the TV while the pastries are cooking and I go into the garden to phone Natalie.

"Hi Alice," she says, "everything OK?"

"All is fine here. How about you? I hope you slept OK?"

"Oh yes, lovely thanks. Your house is so nice."

"It's the same as yours!" I laugh and she does too. "Do you want to stay tonight as well? It will be no bother."

"Oh no, that's fine thank you. We're actually – we're going to go back to Lincoln with Mum."

"Oh. Of course." I feel surprisingly disappointed that she's going. But it makes sense; there is nothing for her to stay for here. And she'll want to be close to her mum, and her brother.

"We'll be back on New Year's Eve," she continues.

"Oh really? I thought you meant you were going back as in moving back."

"Oh no, nothing as dramatic as that. I mean, I don't know yet what I'm going to do, but the kids are happy here. I think I could be too."

"That is great news," I say. "Honestly. And look, if you're back on New Year's Eve, my friends are having a party at the Beach Bar. Family-friendly, lots of lovely kids and nice grown-ups. It's a bit tamer than the wilds of the fancy-dress-filled streets – though if you haven't experienced that yet I'll take you out and show you the sights. We can have a sneaky drink too. I'd better check with Sam but I'm sure he won't mind keeping an eye on the kids for a bit."

"Really?" She sounds so pleased.

"Of course! I will double-check with Becky and Andy, who run the bar, but I am sure they won't mind."

"Thank you Alice, you are single-handedly saving this Christmas."

"I'm really not." I can feel my head swelling. I change the subject. "Has Meg been a good girl?"

"Just perfect. And now Bobby and Courtney want a dog."

"It's not a bad idea!" I say. "If you're staying, and you're home a lot. They're great company." *And great protection too*, I think but keep that thought quiet.

"We're going to leave after lunch, if you don't mind us hanging on till then."

"Of course not. We're still in our pyjamas down here! If you can just let Meg out for a wee again before you go, we'll get back this afternoon." I have a little idea forming in mind of something to do before we go home.

When I go back in, Sam is taking the baking trays out of the oven while he listens to somebody on the other end of the phone, which he has tucked between his shoulder and ear.

"I'll get those," I whisper, taking the tray off him. He puts his hand up to hold his phone properly and straightens his neck, mouthing 'Thanks' and then 'Mum', gesturing with his head to his phone.

"Hi Karen!" I call. I feel really bad that we didn't phone her yesterday. "Thank you for all the presents."

"My pleasure, my love. Happy Christmas!" I hear her voice clearly although she's not on speakerphone. She doesn't seem too put out that we didn't speak yesterday and I soon find out why. "Anyway, Sam, your sister's got something to tell you... she's pregnant!"

"Oh my god!" Sam says. "But I thought you said she wanted to tell me."

"Oh god," says Karen, "don't say I let on, OK?"

I smile at Sam and think of how Shona also blabbed to me about Lydia – who still hasn't told me her news, come to think of it. I'd better phone to thank her properly for our lovely hamper, thus presenting her with the perfect opportunity. This is how it goes, I think; my children are getting older. David and Martin's are nearly adults. Lydia

218

and Si, Jonathan and Janie… this part of life is only just beginning for them.

"OK," Sam says, grinning at me. "But put her on please, Mum."

"Alright, alright." Even from here I can tell Karen is flustered and probably kicking herself for letting the cat out of the bag. "Janie!" she calls and Sam holds his phone away from his ear, wincing.

Soon enough, Janie is on the line, and she tells Sam her news and even though he's already heard it, I see tears forming in his eyes. "That's amazing Janie," he says, the proud big brother. I imagine Ben saying the same to Holly one day.

"Janie's pregnant, Alice," Sam says to me and puts her on speakerphone so I can offer my congratulations too.

"You're going to be an amazing mum!" I say.

"I hope so. I mean, I've wanted this for ages but now it's happening it's scary."

"I know. We know," I say, looking at Sam. "But honestly, you'll be great. And Jon. Send him our love as well please."

"I will. He had to… go for a walk to erm, clear his head today."

I know she doesn't just mean a hangover. Jon, I know of old, is a person who likes his own space and will probably be in need of it after some undiluted Karen time. But I mustn't be too hard on my mother-in-law. She's a good woman really, and she's worked hard to recover her relationship with Sam and Janie.

Sam takes the phone through to Ben and Holly so they can say their thank yous for their presents, so I put the pastries in a basket and place it on the dining room table, then get plates and glasses and some orange squash, which will have to do in place of juice, and soon enough my family come through, children clambering eagerly onto chairs. I take a photo to send to Mum and Dad. I probably ought to tell them they've got house guests.

Eventually, stomachs full of sugary, flaky pastry, we go upstairs to get dressed and repack our bags. I wish we'd brought the car, but not to worry. Maybe I'll go up and get it later, because I want us to do something else first and I am sure after that the children will be practically on their knees. Sam and me too, if I'm honest.

Thankfully, though, everyone is all for my idea and we wrap up warm against what is some genuinely cold and almost Christmassy weather and head down the road towards town. We head off towards the railway station and down to the beach. With the tide out and boots on we can walk out around the rocks and across the wet sand towards the harbour. The water splashes us and we end up semi-soaked despite our coats and boots. There is only one thing for it.

It is busy in the pub but we are lucky enough to find a small table to wedge ourselves into. I sit with Ben and Holly while Sam gets us both a warming rum and coke, and shortly afterwards the barmaid brings over hot chocolates for Ben and Holly.

"What do you say, kids?" Sam prompts.

"Thank you!" they say and she smiles.

We are about to go when we hear an accordion and from the far end of the pub, a bunch of male voices strikes up.

"It's the Sans Day Carol!" I say.

"I'm impressed, Alice," says Sam. "We'll make a Cornish maid of you yet."

"Thank you, I think!"

We stay for the carol but the pub is heaving as more people press in to hear the singers, so we take our leave. Besides, there is not a whole lot of light left in the day. Holly skips ahead of us along the harbourside while Ben saunters casually along behind. I smile at the energy and unfettered childishness of Holly, and at the increasingly self-conscious tween-ness of her brother. Sam and I hold hands and I'm pleased that Ben is not yet at the point of finding this public display of affection beyond the pale. My other hand finds a stone in my pocket: Courtney's Christmas present to me. I hold its smooth shape, feeling it becoming warm between my fingers.

We follow the road around the side of the harbour beach, the end of the pier, and along to the steps which take us past the dog-friendly beach and along to the car park. I quicken my pace but when I look across the tarmac I am disappointed to see that Nigel's van has already gone.

"I hope he's OK," I say to Sam, who squeezes my hand.

"He will be," he says. "And he'll be back, at New Year."

I wonder where Nigel is now. He may not be far away; he's probably being wary of traffic wardens, which is not a bad idea, even on Boxing Day. I walk towards the place where his mobile home had been parked, as though I might find a clue. What I do find on the wall is a collection of stones and shells, arranged in the shape of a heart. I look at it for a moment then I take Courtney's stone from my pocket and place it in the centre, filling the empty space.

Acknowledgements

Well here we are again! Yet another Coming Back to Cornwall book. I now have no idea whether this series will ever end as I've got more storylines swimming around my mind. We'll just see how and where it goes… And I've loved it, writing this new book in the series, and the chance to make it a Christmas episode too. I had originally wondered if I could make it fit more closely to the story of *A Christmas Carol* but it took on a life of its own and ended up a very loose interpretation, so Sam has kindly made the comparison for me, later in the book.

But some of those lessons that can be taken from the Muppets… sorry, the Charles Dickens story, have helped to inspire this book. And it really shouldn't just be at Christmas, although with emotions running high at that time of year it's a good place to start.

I really have my family to thank for the ongoing love and warmth in Alice's family. I realise more and more how lucky I was to grow up in a close, caring and loving home. And my parents were the type of people to invite the Nigels of this world into their home and lives. They were also the type of people to host and attend dinner parties, and I have to mention my Auntie Alice when it comes to buffets because I think hers stand out to me as the most memorable. I used to love family get-togethers, especially at Christmastime. And I do think that the buffet needs a revival.

But back to my 'original' family, the Rogers(es), with whom I have shared so many lovely Christmases. My dad Ted has yet again proofread for me. Dad, it is very special that you show such support for my books and I hope you know how much I appreciate it.

My brothers John and Rich; we are not often all in the same place at the same time these days but when we are it's so good. I love and miss you both. Deb, Jules, Owen, Daniel, Emily and Stan – you are much loved additions to the Rogers family and we are all very lucky to have you (and I've somehow become a Smith).

My mum Rosemary loved Christmas and I am so glad I was able to spend her last one with her and Dad. I am grateful for so much that Mum brought into my life. I miss her every day and even more at special times like this. I think if I had a Christmas wish for myself it would be to go back in time and spend one more Christmas at home with all my family together.

This of course includes my own family now; Chris, Laura and Edward. I'm very lucky to have you and you never fail to inspire me, in my writing and in life in general. I'm looking forward to spending lots more Christmases with you xxx

And now, before I get carried away, my thanks to those other amazing people, who have helped this book to become what it is. Catherine Clarke, I am trying to find new ways of describing you other than just wonderful friend and amazing cover designer. THANK YOU for this amazing cover of a place we both love. Hopefully we will be back there together before too long!

And my super, amazing, fantastic team of beta readers, this time my thanks go to Hilary Kerr, Roz Osborn, Alison Lassey, Rebecca Leech, Sandra Francis, Tracey Shaw, Ginnie Ebbrell, Denise Armstrong, author Nelly Harper, Amanda Tudor, Mandy Chowney-Andrews, Jean Crowe, Ann Bradford, and another author, Marilynn Wrigley. As ever I am worried I'll have left somebody out but I really hope I haven't.

I also wanted to mention that although I have made up the little companies I mention early in the book (and I hope I haven't accidentally nicked any existing company names!), there is one real person I've mentioned, and that is a Bristol artist called Jenny Urquhart, who I have come to know 'virtually' thanks to her mum Pat – hello Pat!

I love Jenny's work and as somebody who used to live in Bristol and still misses it very much, I love seeing all her beautiful paintings of my favourite city. You can find out more about Jenny here: jennyurquhart.co.uk.

And one last hello, and thank you, to Alice at St Ives Bookseller – my favourite bookshop in my favourite place.

OK, I'd better get going and let you all get on with your own Christmases. I really hope you will have enjoyed this return to Cornwall as much as I have and hope to see you all again there soon.

With Christmas wishes and love for the new year,
Kath xx

Coming Back to Cornwall

Books One to Ten

Available in print and on Kindle

The whole Coming Back to Cornwall series is being made into audiobooks so you that you can listen to the adventures of Alice, Julie and Sam while you drive, cook, clean, go to sleep... whatever, wherever! Books One to Five are available now.

Connections
Books One to Four

Each story focuses on a different character all inextricably linked within the small Cornish town they call home.

What Comes Next

An introduction to the Hebden family as they celebrate their first Christmas without much loved wife and mother, Ruth. Set entirely on Christmas Day, at the long barrow where Ruth's ashes have been placed. It is Ruth herself who tells the story, seeing and hearing all.

This short, festive story is an exploration of another side of this time of year normally packed with family, friends and festivities. It is nevertheless uplifting and engaging, and full of Christmas spirit.

The first full-length novel begins with an illicit kiss, with Ruth its only witness but unable to say or do anything about it. As her family begin to find their way through their grief and navigate new situations and changing relationships, Ruth herself has much to learn as she comes to terms  with her new situation and the fact that she can now only watch as life moves on without her.

Individual novels

Writing the Town Read: Katharine's first novel. "I seriously couldn't put it down and would recommend it to anyone who doesn't like chick lit, but wants a great story."

Looking Past - a story of motherhood and growing up without a mother.

"Despite the tough topic the book is full of love, friendships and humour. Katharine Smith cleverly balances emotional storylines with strong characters and witty dialogue, making this a surprisingly happy book to read."

Amongst Friends - a back-to-front tale of friendship and family, set in Bristol.

"An interesting, well written book, set in Bristol which is lovingly described, and with excellent characterisation. Very enjoyable."

Printed in Great Britain
by Amazon

52548727R00137